A Presidential Exception

When they reached the front gates of the White House, Clint was looking out the window. The gates were opened by two guards, who waved them through without asking for any identification.

The cab stopped in front of the White House and the driver dropped down and opened the door for Clint.

"Thank you."

As Clint stepped down, two armed soldiers approached.

"Mr. Adams?" one of them asked.

"That's right."

"Sir, we'll need your weapon."

Normally, Clint would have refused such a request, but this was a meeting with the President of the United States in the White House. If that wasn't an exception, he didn't know what was.

D0814220

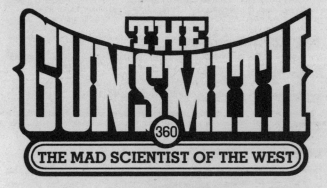

THE GUNSMITH

360

THE MAD SCIENTIST OF THE WEST

J. R. ROBERTS

JOVE BOOKS, NEW YORK

THE BERKLEY PUBLISHING GROUP
Published by the Penguin Group
Penguin Group (USA) Inc.
375 Hudson Street, New York, New York 10014, USA
Penguin Group (Canada), 90 Eglinton Avenue East, Suite 700, Toronto, Ontario M4P 2Y3, Canada
(a division of Pearson Penguin Canada Inc.)
Penguin Books Ltd., 80 Strand, London WC2R 0RL, England
Penguin Group Ireland, 25 St. Stephen's Green, Dublin 2, Ireland (a division of Penguin Books Ltd.)
Penguin Group (Australia), 250 Camberwell Road, Camberwell, Victoria 3124, Australia
(a division of Pearson Australia Group Pty. Ltd.)
Penguin Books India Pvt. Ltd., 11 Community Centre, Panchsheel Park, New Delhi—110 017, India
Penguin Group (NZ), 67 Apollo Drive, Rosedale, Auckland 0632, New Zealand
(a division of Pearson New Zealand Ltd.)
Penguin Books (South Africa) (Pty.) Ltd., 24 Sturdee Avenue, Rosebank, Johannesburg 2196,
South Africa

Penguin Books Ltd., Registered Offices: 80 Strand, London WC2R 0RL, England

This is a work of fiction. Names, characters, places, and incidents either are the product of the author's imagination or are used fictitiously, and any resemblance to actual persons, living or dead, business establishments, events, or locales is entirely coincidental

THE MAD SCIENTIST OF THE WEST

A Jove Book / published by arrangement with the author

PRINTING HISTORY
Jove edition / December 2011

ISBN: 978-0-515-15020-9

JOVE®
Jove Books are published by The Berkley Publishing Group,
a division of Penguin Group (USA) Inc.,
375 Hudson Street, New York, New York 10014.
JOVE® is a registered trademark of Penguin Group (USA) Inc.
The "J" design is a trademark of Penguin Group (USA) Inc.

PRINTED IN THE UNITED STATES OF AMERICA

10 9 8 7 6 5 4 3 2 1

ONE

Clint Adams had been to the White House several times, but it had been a few years. His last few trips to Washington, D.C., had involved the government, but did not involve seeing the President directly.

Grover Cleveland was in the midst of his first term. Clint had already met this President, but had not seen him for some time when he received the summons to appear. It might have been a request, but Clint would have responded to either one.

He arrived in Washington the day before he was to meet with the President. He got himself registered in the hotel on Q Street, then went out and got himself a good steak. He had some friends in Washington, but had not contacted any of them. And he wouldn't, not until he found out what the President wanted with him.

After dinner he went back to his room and spent the rest of the evening reading. The next morning he had breakfast in the hotel dining room, then stepped out in front of the hotel to wait.

"Sir?" the doorman asked.

"I'm waiting for a cab that's been sent to pick me up," Clint said.

"Yes, sir."

When the hansom cab pulled up in front of the hotel, the doorman obviously recognized it. The two American flags on either side might have been a hint for him. The driver sat in front of the enclosed cab rather than behind it.

"Sir!" he said to Clint. "Your cab is here."

"Thank you."

The doorman beat Clint to the cab and opened the door for him. Clint stepped inside, then tried to tip the doorman, who waved his large, white-gloved hand.

"No, sir, not necessary," the man said. "Have a good day."

"Thanks, you, too."

The doorman closed the door, then slapped his hand on the side of the cab and shouted, "Driver!"

The cab started off, and Clint was left inside, alone with his thoughts.

When they reached the front gates of the White House, Clint was looking out the window. The gates were opened by two guards, who waved them through without asking for any identification.

The cab stopped in front of the White House, and the driver dropped down and opened the door for Clint.

"Thank you."

As Clint stepped down, two armed soldiers approached.

"Mr. Adams?" one of them asked.

"That's right."

"Sir, we'll need your weapon."

Normally, Clint would have refused such a request, but

this was a meeting with the President of the United States in the White House. If that wasn't an exception, he didn't know what was.

He handed over his gun.

"Thank you, sir," one of the soldiers said. "Follow us, please."

Actually, he followed one soldier, while the other walked behind him. They marched him into the White House, where a man in a suit was waiting for him. He was a florid-faced man in his forties, in good shape except for a slightly prominent belly his suit had been expensively cut to accommodate.

"Mr. Adams? I'm Wallace Cromartie. I'm to take you to the President."

"Thanks."

"This way, please."

This time the two soldiers walked behind him as he walked alongside Cromartie.

"May I ask what your position is, Mr. Cromartie?"

"Certainly," Cromartie said. "I'm a sort of special advisor to the President."

"Special advisor? For what kind of things?"

"Well . . . the kind of thing that would bring a man such as yourself to the White House," Cromartie said. Which really didn't answer the question at all.

They walked down several hallways, past more soldiers, until they reached the doors to the Oval Office.

"Wait here, please," Cromartie said.

Clint waited with the two soldiers while Cromartie went inside. Clint thought idly that if this was a trick to disarm him so he would be a sitting duck, it would be an elaborate one.

The door opened again and Cromartie said, "The President will see you now, Mr. Adams."

TWO

President Grover Cleveland filled the room, even though he was seated behind his desk. About fifty, he was a large man with a majestic mustache—or what some people called "mustaches."

"Clint Adams," the President said, rising. "Welcome. May I call you Clint?"

"Of course, sir."

Cleveland came around the desk and met Clint in the center of the room with a crushing handshake.

"Okay, Warren," he said to Cromartie. "You can go."

"I, uh, thought I'd sit in—"

"Perhaps later," Cleveland said. "I'd like to see Clint alone for a while."

"Of course, sir," Cromartie said, and left the room.

"You allowed them to disarm you," the President said. "I'm sorry about that, but—"

"That's all right, sir," Clint said. "I understand the need for security."

"Yes, of course you do. Please, sit," he said, indicating the sofas in the center of the room, with a low table separating them.

Clint chose a sofa, and the President sat across from him.

"Hotel okay?"

"Yes, sir."

"And your trip? And transportation here?"

"All first class, sir. No complaints."

"Good, good."

The door opened and a white-gloved man entered carrying a silver tray with a coffeepot and china cups on it.

"I arranged for some coffee. Unless you'd like something stronger?"

"No, sir," Clint said. "Coffee is fine."

"All right, Henry," Cleveland said.

The man set the tray down on the table that separated Clint from Cleveland. He poured two cups, then looked at the President.

"That's fine," Cleveland said. "We'll take care of the sugar and cream ourselves."

"Yes, sir."

Henry withdrew from the room.

"Help yourself," Cleveland said.

"Just black is fine with me," Clint said, picking up the cup.

Cleveland poured in cream from a small pitcher and then added several sugar cubes. He stirred, then picked up his cup and sat back.

"Nikola Tesla," he said. "Do you know the name?"

"I've heard of him, yes," Clint said. "Some people call him a mad scientist."

"That may very well be true," Cleveland said, "but he's brilliant, nevertheless. His work with electricity may very well be priceless to our country."

"And what about Thomas Edison?"

"Also brilliant, but impossible to deal with. He and Tesla have an adversarial relationship at best."

"I see."

Clint sipped his coffee and waited for the President to get to the point.

Cleveland drank some coffee and then set the cup down.

"Mr. Adams—Clint—we believe that Tesla's life is in danger. I would like you to make sure that he does not get killed."

"You want me to be his bodyguard?"

"Exactly."

"You think Edison is trying to have him killed?"

"Not at all," Cleveland said. "Edison may be a pain in the butt, but he's no killer. No, we don't know who's behind it. We've got somebody working on that part of it. I believe you know him? Jim West?"

"Yes, a good friend of mine. Did he recommend me for this?"

"As a matter of fact, he did," Cleveland said, "but I had already started to think about you. It was just a case of great minds thinking alike."

Clint had heard his friend West described many ways, but never as a great mind. That kind of thing was usually reserved for people like Edison and Tesla.

"Of course, you'll be paid for your time," Cleveland said.

"That's not a concern, sir," Clint said. "If you want me to do this, I'll do it."

"That was what West said you'd say, but we'll pay you. If you like, we'll just deposit the money into your account until the job is over."

"That'll be fine. Where is Tesla now?"

"Colorado," Cleveland said. "He plans to do some experimenting in the mountains, but you can join him in Denver."

"When, sir?"

"As soon as possible."

"I can probably get on a train this afternoon, or at least tomorrow morning."

"You already have a ticket for this afternoon's train."

"Am I that predictable?"

"You'll have to ask your friend West about that," Cleveland said. "He's the one who told me to go ahead and buy the ticket."

Both men stood.

"You can keep in contact with me by telegraph," the President said. "Mr. Cromartie will give you all the details."

"Yes, sir."

The President extended his hand, and Clint shook it firmly.

"I appreciate the help, Clint," the man said.

"It's my pleasure, sir," Clint said. "I'm always ready to help my country."

"Mr. Cromartie should be right outside the door," Cleveland, moving back to his desk. "I have some paperwork to get back to. He has your ticket, the rest of the facts, and he'll see you out."

"Yes, sir," Clint said. "I'll be in touch."

"One other thing, Clint," the President said.

"What's that?"

"When Tesla gets something in his head, he gets sort of . . . well, focused. Fixed. He loses any sense of . . . propriety."

"And?"

"I need you to keep him out of trouble," Cleveland said. "Don't let him do anything that might get him . . ."

"Arrested? Killed?"

"And more," Cleveland said. "Just keep him out of trouble."

"Yes, sir."

By the time Clint went out the door, Grover Cleveland's attention was on something else.

THREE

Clint left the White House, escorted every step of the way at first by Cromartie, and then by two soldiers. Once outside he found a telegraph office and sent a telegram to his friend Rick Hartman, in Labyrinth, Texas. He had traveled by stage and rail, and in doing so had left Eclipse behind in Rick's care. He just wanted to let his friend know where he'd be. He promised in his telegram to drop another line when he knew where he would be in Colorado.

From there he returned to his hotel, packed, and barely made his train.

Clint made good time, arriving in Denver three-and-a-half days later, despite the trains stopping for water, and time lost changing trains. As soon as he arrived, he headed right to the Denver House Hotel, where he always stayed when he was in town.

Their turnover of clerks must have been amazing. He never seemed to see the same desk clerk when he arrived, and yet they always said, "Glad to have you back," when he checked in.

"Can I have someone take your bag?" the man asked.

"No, thanks," Clint said. "I've got it." He had only one carpetbag with him. He picked it up and carried it to his room.

He had already telegraphed from Washington to see if his friend Talbot Roper was in town. Roper was a private investigator, the best in the country, and a longtime friend. He received a message back from Roper's current secretary saying he was out of town.

So there was nothing to do but meet with Tesla.

According to Cromartie, Tesla was in a Market Street hotel called the Bijou. When Clint got down from the cab, he saw that the hotel and the neighborhood were both run-down, even seedy. There were some beggars out front as he entered, and he had to wake the desk clerk to ask for Tesla's room.

"He may have a girl with him, though," the clerk said. "Maybe you should wait."

"That's okay," Clint said. "He's expecting me."

"Suit yerself."

Clint went up the stairs to Room 5 and knocked.

A slender man with a carefully manicured mustache opened the door.

"Yes?"

"Mr. Tesla? I'm Clint Adams."

The man stared at him for a few moments, then said, "Oh, my bodyguard, right?"

"Right."

"Come in, come in," Tesla said.

Clint entered. The first thing he saw was a girl sitting in a chair. She was naked to the waist, and there were some wires hooked to the nipples of her small breasts. He followed the wires to a box with some dials on it, and on top some metal rods with wires wrapped around them.

"What's going on?" he asked.

"Oh, this?" Tesla asked. "This is Angela. She's agreed to help me with some experiments."

The girl stared up at Clint with a glassy smile. He saw an empty whiskey bottle on a table next to her.

"Just watch what happens when I flip this switch," Tesla said.

"You got her drunk so she'd do this?" Clint asked.

"Well," Tesla said, "I just needed her to loosen up a little."

As Tesla approached the box to flip the switch, the girl giggled.

"Okay, hold it," Clint said. He put himself between Tesla and the box. "Forget that."

"What?"

"Part of my job, Mr. Tesla, is to keep you out of trouble."

"I'm not getting into trouble."

"If you hurt this girl, you will be."

Clint removed the wires from the top of the box, then went to the girl. She had abnormally large, distended nipples, and Tesla had wrapped the thin wires around them.

"Jesus," Clint said. "Doesn't that hurt?"

She looked up at him and said, "It kind of tickles."

Clint knelt in front of her and unwound the wires from her nipples.

"We goin' to bed now?" she asked. "All of us?"

Her shirt was hung over the back of her chair, so Clint grabbed it and draped it over her.

"Sorry," he told her, "nobody's going to bed tonight."

He got her to her feet and pushed her toward the door.
She wasn't too drunk to ask, "Am I still gettin' paid?"
"Sure you are," Tesla said. He looked at Clint. "Pay her."
"That's not part of my job," Clint told him.
Tesla grinned.
"It was worth a try."
He paid the girl, and she left.

FOUR

"I was just doing an experiment," Tesla said.

"On a live person?" Clint asked. "Is that wise?"

"Did you see her nipples?"

They were sitting at a table in a steakhouse that Tesla had recommended. Given the hotel Tesla had chosen to stay in, Clint wasn't sure about his choice of restaurant, but it turned out to be excellent.

"I don't think the President would be happy to hear you were using live prostitutes for your experiments."

"Well," Tesla said, cutting himself a hunk of steak, "we don't have to tell him, do we?"

"I work for the man," Clint said.

Tesla put the steak in his mouth and then pointed across the table with his fork.

"You're the Gunsmith, right?"

"Right."

"I heard you were your own man."

"That's true," Clint said. "I'm also a man who's loyal to his country, and his President."

"Well," Tesla said, going back to his steak, "I can see you're going to be a lot of fun to have around."

"Is that what this is supposed to be all about?" Clint asked. "Fun?"

"No, it's about electricity," Tesla said. "What do you know about it?"

"Just that Ben Franklin flew a kite."

"Wow," Tesla said, "I am tired of hearing about that. Do you know anything about alternating current?"

"Not a thing," Clint said. "Do you know anything about somebody wanting to kill you?"

"Not a thing," Tesla said. "I've seen no evidence of that rumor."

"The President feels it's more than a rumor."

"The only person I can think of who would benefit from my death is Thomas Edison," Tesla said, "and I cannot see Thomas going to that extent. We may not be friends, but I won't believe that of him."

"Then maybe it's someone else."

"Like who?"

"Oh, I don't know," Clint said. "How many other women have you tried to experiment on? Maybe somebody's boyfriend or husband is after you?"

"I doubt it," Tesla said. "This was a first. I've never attached wires to the nipples of a woman before. That's what made it so appealing."

"Appealing?" Clint asked. "I didn't see anything appealing about it."

"You're right," Tesla said. "She didn't have very good breasts. But she did have marvelous nipples."

"Eat your steak," Clint said, "and tell me why you're staying in that hotel."

"I like it."

"I'm sure the government would provide you with better lodgings," Clint said.

"I like to make my own arrangements."

"Money, then."

"I have my own."

"I see," Clint said.

"Do you?" Tesla asked. "You see, much like yourself, I like to be my own man."

"I can understand that," Clint said, "but the government—"

"Has no claim on my work," Tesla said. "They're interested in my work, but they have no claim on it."

"Then who does?"

"Me," Tesla said. "Just me."

FIVE

Tesla told Clint he was leaving Denver the next day.

"Where are we going?"

"We?"

"It's my job to stick with you," Clint said. "Where you go, I go."

"Well, we're going up higher—above Gunnison."

"Littleton?"

"You know the area?"

"Yes."

"Well, not as far as Littleton," Tesla said. "There's a house between the two towns. That's where we're going. Out in the middle of nowhere."

"You bought the house?"

Tesla shook his head.

"I am renting it."

"You got supplies?"

"I am having them delivered," Tesla said. "Everything should either be there when we arrive, or get there soon after."

"Supplies, food stores, water . . ."

"Everything I need," Tesla said.

Clint wasn't sure that meant everything that he needed, as well.

They left the restaurant and got into a cab. Clint told the driver to take them to the Denver House.

"Excuse me?" Tesla said. "Everything I own is at the Bijou."

"And my stuff is at the Denver House. We'll pick it up and then I'll go back to the Bijou with you."

"Is that necessary?"

"Like I said over dinner," Clint reminded him, "I go where you go."

"You're not going to share my room."

"Don't worry, I'll get my own."

"What if there are no more rooms?"

"Don't worry," Clint said. "I'll get one."

At the Denver House, Clint made sure Tesla went in with him. First, he didn't want the man running away. Second, maybe seeing the place would convince the man to stay there.

It didn't.

"Nice room," Tesla said as Clint collected his belongings, "but I like mine better. More character."

"You're probably right."

They went back down to the lobby, where Clint checked out.

"Leaving already?" the clerk said. "Come back soon, sir."

"Thanks."

They went back out to their cab and took it to the Bijou.

Clint got a room right across from Tesla's.

"Leave your door open," Clint said, fitting the key into his lock.

"What are you afraid I'll do?" Tesla asked.

"Get killed."

Tesla left his door open.

Tesla appeared at Clint's open door sometime later, holding a bottle of whiskey and two glasses.

"Drink?"

Clint looked up from the book he was reading.

"I prefer beer."

Tesla wagged the bottle back and forth.

"If you let me drink alone, I'm liable to do something stupid."

Clint put the Mark Twain book down and swung his feet off the bed to the floor.

"In that case, I'll join you."

"Excellent!"

Tesla entered, closing the door behind him. He poured two glasses full and handed one to Clint. The filled glasses represented half a dozen shots.

"Thanks."

Tesla saw the Twain on the bed and gave Clint an interested look.

"A gunman who reads?"

"I'm not a gunman."

"But your reputation—"

"An intelligent man like you should know better than to believe everything he reads or hears."

Tesla stared at Clint again, then sipped his drink and said, "I'm sorry."

"What if I believed everything I heard about you?" Clint asked. "I'd think you were some kind of mad scientist."

"Well, in my case that wouldn't be far from the truth," Tesla admitted.

Clint studied the young man, who looked as if he was not yet thirty.

"All right, then," Clint said. "I'll admit I'm good with a gun, and I've used it to kill men, but only when there was no other way to resolve an issue—or if they deserved it."

"Where are you from?" Tesla asked.

"I was born in the East, but have spent my life in the West," was all Clint would say. "And you?"

"Serbia," Tesla said, "but I quickly outgrew my village, Smiljan. I left, traveled, and found my way to the United States, where I could pursue my work."

"Could there be somebody from home who means you harm?" Clint asked.

"I doubt it," Tesla said. "I truly don't know of anyone who'd mean me harm. I believe your President is overreacting to some rumors he may have heard."

"Well, they have a man trying to track down the source and find out if the threat is real," Clint said.

"Meanwhile, you will keep me safe."

"Yes."

"A toast, then," Tesla said, raising his glass, "to being safe."

Clint raised his glass and echoed the sentiment.

"To being safe."

The two men drank, and then Tesla headed for the door.

"I'll go back to my room and let you continue with your reading," he said. "I have some thinking to do. I'll see you in the morning. Early."

"How are we traveling?"

"We are taking some supplies with us, so by wagon," Tesla said. "It will be waiting outside for us."

"Very good."

"A quick breakfast," Tesla said, "and then we shall be off."

He said good night to Clint, and then went across the hall to his own room, closing the door behind him. Clint's door remained open.

He noticed that Tesla had taken the whiskey bottle with him.

SIX

In the morning Clint found Nikola Tesla waiting in the seat of a buckboard, with a team of two. The bed behind him seemed loaded for bear and was covered with a tarp.

"Good morning!"

Tesla seemed wide-eyed and awake, and Clint assumed he had not finished off that entire bottle of whiskey by himself.

"Morning," Clint said.

"Toss your belongings in the back, if you can find room," Tesla said.

Clint lifted the tarp and stuffed his bag underneath, then joined Tesla in the seat.

"What about breakfast?" he asked. "You promised me breakfast."

"Just down the block," Tesla said, "Same place we had the steak last night."

"That suits me," Clint said.

Nikola Tesla drove the buckboard half a block, long enough for Clint to see that the man knew how to handle a team.

Sitting across a table from Tesla, having breakfast with him, Clint could see that his eyes were very clear, further indication that he had not drunk all the whiskey last night.

Or he was an extraordinary drinker.

"Don't you usually need some kind of assistant for your experiments?" Clint asked over his plate of steak and eggs.

"No," Tesla said, "but if I do need an assistant over the next week or so, you'll be there."

"As long as you don't try to attach wires to my nipples," Clint said, "I'll try to help you as much as I can."

"I think you're safe," Tesla said.

"Good."

"Maybe I'll even make a scientist out of you," Tesla said.

"I'll be satisfied just to be a good assistant," Clint said.

"Actually," Tesla said, "I suppose I would be happy if you were just a good bodyguard."

"I guess we'll find out."

After breakfast they climbed aboard the wagon and headed out.

"Just to be on the safe side," Clint said, "you did bring enough supplies for us to camp along the way, didn't you?"

"I did," Tesla said. "I'm not a fool, Clint. I realize this is a long trip, and we will need to set up camp as we travel."

"Like I said," Clint pointed out, "I was just checking. It's going to take us the better part of two weeks to get up there, and I want to make sure we'll be able to eat."

"Won't we come across other towns?" Tesla asked.

"Some settlements, maybe," Clint said. "But we should make sure we're outfitted to make it all the way, just in case."

Tesla swallowed and said, "Uh, well, maybe we should make one more stop before we leave, then. Just to be on the safe side."

"Sure thing," Clint said, "just to be on the safe side."

SEVEN

They stopped at a mercantile store and Clint stocked up on canned goods and coffee, as well as some beef jerky. By the time he got the supplies stowed in the back of the buckboard, he couldn't have gotten a cigar in there.

"What is all that stuff back there?" he asked, climbing back in the seat next to Tesla.

"Those are my supplies," Tesla said. "What I'll need for my experiments."

"And why are we going all the way to where we're going to do those experiments?"

"Because I need altitude," Tesla said, "and that's about as high as I can figure."

"Can't argue with that," Clint said. "We're certainly going to get some altitude going up past Gunnison."

"That's exactly why I chose this house," Tesla told him.

A full day's ride outside of Denver, already at a higher altitude, they reined the team in and stopped for the night.

Clint suggested an earlier stop than Tesla had planned, so they could get their fire built before nightfall.

"Don't want to break an ankle while we're out looking for firewood," he said. His main concern was that Tesla was a city boy, not used to being on the trail. If anyone was gong to break an ankle, it would be him, if he didn't wander too far away from camp and get lost first.

As it turned out, Tesla was very adept at making camp, finding firewood, building a fire, and was even good with the horses.

"My village in Serbia was in the middle of nowhere," he told Clint as they sat around the fire. "The terrain was much like this. So I am not the—what is the word: tenderfoot?—I am not the tenderfoot that you feared I would be."

"My apologies for underestimating you," Clint said. "I won't do it again."

It was Clint who made the coffee and the beans, handed a plate across to Tesla, and then a cup of coffee.

"Thank you."

"When we get up to the house you rented, I can go out and hunt up some meat for us."

"That would be good," Tesla said. "By the time we arrive, I will probably be tired of beans."

"I bought some bacon," Clint said. "I can mix that in next time."

They pulled their coats tightly around them as the temperature continued to drop. Thank God it wasn't winter, so they wouldn't have to deal with snow.

When they'd finished eating, Clint double-checked the horses to make sure they were secure, then returned to the fire to make another pot of coffee.

"No more for me," Tesla said.

"I'll be drinking it while I'm on watch," Clint said.

"You are not going to sleep?"

"I didn't notice anyone following us," Clint said, "but it is my job to keep you safe, so I'll be on watch all night."

"But . . . when will you sleep?"

"I can doze while you drive the buckboard," Clint said.

Normally Clint would have depended on his Darley Arabian, Eclipse, to alert him to trouble, so he could have dozed while on watch.

"I will take a second watch," Tesla said. "It would not be fair to you for you to stay awake all night."

"Can you shoot?"

"With a rifle, yes. Perhaps not well, but yes."

"Well," Clint said, "you'll just have to sit with it across your knees. If you see anything, or hear anything, you can just wake me."

"Fine," Tesla said. "I can do that. I'll also be looking at the sky."

"Part of your experiment?" Clint asked.

"Research," Tesla said.

"Well, I may not have to tell you this, but make sure you don't look into the fire."

"Night vision," Tesla said. "Yes, I know."

"Well," Clint said, "apparently you know a lot more about what goes on in my life than I know about you and yours."

"Electricity?" Tesla said. "I can teach you."

"I doubt it."

"We'll see," Tesla said. "When we get to the house. For now, I'll get some sleep."

"I'll wake you in four hours."

"See you then," Tesla said.

He rolled himself up in his blanket and was almost immediately asleep.

EIGHT

When his watch was over, Clint fell asleep and was out until morning, waking up to the smell of bacon frying. Apparently, cooking on the trail was also one of Tesla's talents.

The coffee wasn't strong enough, but Clint decided not to mention it. The bacon was good.

"Didn't hear or see a thing all night," Tesla announced over breakfast. "Maybe there's no one trying to kill me, after all."

"Or maybe they know where we're going, so they don't have to follow us," Clint suggested. "Who else knows about this house?"

"No one," Tesla said. "Until you arrived, I was a one-man operation."

"Well, you rented it from someone, so somebody knows where we're going."

"That is not very encouraging," Tesla said.

"Sorry. I just have to be ready for any eventuality," Clint explained.

"I am the same way with my experiments," Tesla said, "so I understand."

After breakfast they broke camp and Tesla hitched the horses up to the buckboard. Clint resisted the urge to check that they were firmly hitched. Tesla seemed to know what he was doing when it came to horses and buckboards and making and breaking camp.

Clint hoped he was as good at his own things, as well, and that the government was going to get what they hoped for.

"So, what did the President tell you about me?" Tesla asked.

"Have you met him?"

"Me?" Tesla looked surprised. "Meet President Cleveland? No."

"Really?"

"Does that surprise you?"

"He spoke as if he knew you."

"Well, perhaps he knows me," Tesla offered, "but I do not know him. However, I'm sure we will meet sometime in the future."

"I'd think so," Clint said. "He seems to think your experiments could mean a lot to the country."

"Harnessing electricity and bending it to our will could benefit the entire world," Tesla said. "So, what did he tell you about me?"

"He said you might be a mad scientist, but you were important."

"Mad, perhaps," Tesla said. "Certainly a scientist. Important? You have no idea."

NINE

The second night on the trail passed without incident. They split the watch again, and covered good ground on day three. Toward night they saw some smoke ahead.

"Stop," Clint said.

Tesla reined the two-horse team in.

"Someone making camp?"

"I don't think so," Clint said. "Not unless they made more than one fire. I'm thinking it's some kind of settlement ahead."

"Does that pose a danger to us?" Tesla asked.

"One never knows," Clint said.

Tesla turned his head and regarded Clint.

"I suppose when you enter any town, you have to wonder what is waiting for you there."

"Pretty much."

"It must be a hard life. Why did you choose it?"

"I didn't," Clint said. "It chose me."

They sat in silence for a few moments, looking ahead at the plumes of smoke.

"So what shall we do?"

"We ride through," Clint said.

"What if it's a settlement with a saloon, or restaurant? I could use something other than beans and bacon."

"We've only been on the trail for two nights," Clint said.

"Yes, well," Tesla said apologetically, "I've never been very good at roughing it."

"I thought you said your village was like this?" Clint asked.

"Yes, it was," Tesla said, "but I have been away from there a very long time."

"All right, then," Clint said. "Let's just go ahead and see what happens."

Eventually they came to a road—not a well-traveled one, but one that had seen some recent use. They took it and reached the source of the smoke plumes—a settlement made up of tents and falling-down shacks. There were several fires going, and a couple of the shacks had some smoke coming from pipe chimneys.

As they drove in, they became the center of attention. People stopped what they were doing to watch them drive by.

"Where should we go?" Tesla asked.

"That biggest tent," Clint said, pointing.

When they passed one tent, several women came out, showing their wares.

"Whores," Clint said. "Looks like a small mining town."

"How do you know?"

"Mining towns attract whores, gamblers, and worse."

"What is worse?"

"Con men, killers."

"Ah," Tesla said. "Perhaps we should not stop, after all. We really don't need any supplies."

"Let's just ask how far we are from Gunnison," Clint said. "Then we can keep on. We've still got a few hours of daylight."

They passed another tent, and three men came out to take a look. They all had whiskey glasses in their hands. They wore dirty trail clothes, guns in worn holsters, and hungry looks.

"They do not look very welcoming," Tesla said.

"We'll have to watch them," Clint said. "They look like the types who think they're entitled."

"To what?"

"Whatever they want."

Tesla halted the team in front of the large tent. The flap was open. Clint could see that the inside was filled with shelves of supplies.

"Trading post," he said, "or a general store."

Tesla turned, saw the three men still staring after them.

"Where's your rifle?" Clint asked.

Tesla reached beneath the seat, came out with a Winchester.

"Okay, I'm going in to ask about Gunnison," Clint said. "Keep watch. If you think there's going to be trouble, fire off a shot. I'll come running."

"Fire a shot . . . where?" Tesla asked.

"Straight up," Clint said, pointing. "Into the air."

Tesla looked straight up, then back at Clint.

"When you do that," he asked, "where does the bullet go?"

"Up."

"But . . . where does it end up?"

"Nikola," Clint said, "we'll do an experiment later, okay?"

Tesla looked nervous and said, "Okay."

TEN

When Clint entered the tent, he saw that it was filled with supplies set on floor-to-ceiling homemade shelves. Off to one side was a similarly handmade counter, behind which a morose-looking man stood.

"Buyin'?" the man asked.

"No."

"Sellin'?"

"Sorry," Clint said.

"I'd advise you not to leave your wagon out there, then," the man said. "Too many fellas around here with sticky fingers."

"I got a man on the wagon."

"Hope he's got a gun."

"He does."

"Hope he can use it."

"Well," Clint said, "I've only got one question and then we'll be on our way."

"Go ahead and ask."

"Gunnison," Clint said. "How far away are we?"

"A day's ride," the man said.

"Buckboard or by horse?" Clint asked.

"You stay to the road, you should be able to make it with your buckboard."

"Okay," Clint said, "thanks."

"Sure you don't need somethin' before you go?" the man asked.

"No," Clint said, "we're pretty well set."

"Where you comin' from?"

"Denver."

"Two nights on the trail?"

"That's right."

"Well," the man said, "you should make Gunnison easy. They got a general store there."

"That's good to know," Clint said. "Thanks."

Clint nodded, turned, and walked out the tent flap. Outside he saw that the three men who had been watching them now had the wagon surrounded. One of them was holding Tesla's rifle, had apparently taken it away from the scientist before he could fire a shot. Clint looked around, saw a barrel filled with hickory ax handles.

"Any law in this town?" he asked the storekeeper.

"Just what you can enforce yerself," the man said.

He grabbed one of the ax handles and stepped forward . . .

Tesla was surprised at how quickly the three men had surrounded him, suddenly yanking the rifle from his hand before he could fire a warning shot for Clint.

"Give that back!" he shouted to the man holding his rifle.

"Now, that ain't exactly friendly," one of the men said. "Sittin' there with a rifle over yer knees. Whataya think, Donnie?"

"Not friendly at all," Donnie said.

Tesla couldn't tell the three men apart; they looked the same to him. Same clothes, same stubble on their faces, same hard expressions on their face.

"What do you want?" he demanded.

The third man walked to the back of the buckboard and peered under the tarp.

"Whoeee, boys, but he got a lot of stuff under here," he called out.

"Don't touch that!" Tesla yelled. "Some of it is delicate."

"Delicate, ya say?" the first man said. "Then maybe you need to have it protected."

"We could do that," the one called Donnie said. "Hey, Roman?"

The first man—Roman—said, "We sure could, fer a price."

"I don't need to have it protected," Tesla said.

"Yeah, ya do," the third man said. "'Cause otherwise somethin' could get broke."

"Yeah," Roman said, "you need protection, dude."

Tesla suddenly saw Clint coming out of the tent and felt relief flood over him.

"I already have protection," he said.

"And where would that be?" Roman asked.

"Right behind you."

Roman turned his head, saw the man coming out of the tent carrying an ax handle, and turned to face him. The other two men also saw the man and stepped away from the wagon . . .

"Can I help you fellows with something?" Clint asked.

"This your wagon?" Roman asked.

"It is."

"Where you headed?"

"North."

"Gunnison?"

"That direction."

Roman jerked his thumb at the buckboard.

"This stuff valuable?"

"It has value to us," Clint said.

"Seems to me ya may need some protection, then," Roman said.

"You fellas hire out for that sort of thing?"

"We do."

"Well," Clint said, "I think we're okay. Why don't you give my friend back his rifle?"

"I don't know," Roman said, "he might get hurt."

Clint moved closer, keeping the ax handle down by his leg, in his left hand.

"I don't think he will," he said. "Just hand it back to him and we'll be on our way."

"Without protection?"

"We've got protection."

"Just you?"

"I'm enough."

Roman exchanged a glance with his cohorts. Clint took the opportunity to move even closer. He thought he was now within reach with the ax handle.

ELEVEN

"Yer pushin' it, friend," Roman said.

Clint lunged forward with the ax handle and buried it in the man's stomach. As Roman doubled over, Clint snatched the rifle from his hand and tossed it back to Tesla, who reacted just in time to catch it.

"Don't," Clint said, pointing with the ax handle at the other men.

"Yer makin' a big mistake, mister," Donnie said.

Roman straightened up and went for his gun. Clint swung the ax handle again, got the man on the forearm before he could draw his gun. There was a loud crack as the bone in his arm broke, and then Roman was holding his arm and howling.

"This town got a doctor?" Clint asked the other two men.

"Yeah—" Donnie started.

"Better get your friend over there," Clint said. "We're going to be on our way. I hope we don't cross paths again."

"You better hope that," the third man said.

He and Donnie moved to either side of Roman and helped him away from the buckboard. They looked back over their shoulders a couple of times before they committed to taking Roman to the doctor.

"That may not have been a good idea," the storekeeper said to Clint from behind.

Clint turned and held the ax handle out to the man to give it back.

"Keep it," the man said. "You're pretty good with it."

"Thanks."

Clint climbed up next to Tesla, set the ax handle beneath the seat, where Tesla had also replaced the rifle.

"I'm sorry," Tesla said. "They surprised me."

"It's okay," Clint said. "Let's just get moving before they come back with help."

Tesla flicked the reins at the team.

"How far do we have to go?" he asked as they pulled away from the settlement.

"A day's drive," Clint said. "We probably need one more night on the trail, and then we'll reach Gunnison tomorrow. How much farther will the house be after that?"

"A few hours, according to the man I rented it from," Tesla said.

"Who did you rent it from anyway?"

"An agency," Tesla said. "I saw the ad in the Denver newspaper."

An agency, not an individual. That meant any one of a few people could give away their location.

He turned and looked behind them, saw that at the moment no one was following.

"Do you expect more trouble from those fellows?" Tesla asked.

"I guess that depends on how badly I hurt that man's arm."

"I thought I heard a bone crack."

"So did I."

"So if he's that hurt, he won't come after us."

"Just the opposite," Clint said. "If I broke his arm, he's going to want his revenge."

"Well, I assume you can handle them," Tesla said. "You certainly did just now."

"We'll have to see," Clint said.

"Why didn't you shoot that man when he tried to draw his gun?"

"I didn't feel I needed to," Clint said. "I'm not anxious to kill a man at any time, but I don't even know this one. Hopefully, he learned his lesson and we're done with him and his friends."

"I hope so."

They traveled a few hours more and then stopped to set up camp.

"Sorry we couldn't get a meal back there before leaving," Clint said, handing Tesla a plate of beans.

"Don't worry about it," the scientist said. "I was just glad to get away from there."

"The storekeeper there said there's a general store in Gunnison," Clint said. "We should be able to go back and forth when we need supplies."

"I have everything I need for my experiments," Tesla said, "except for a few other things that will be delivered. Other than that, we'd just need food and coffee and other sundries."

"Shouldn't be a problem," Clint said. "Not if there's a store in Gunnison."

"What about those fellows from back there?" Tesla asked.

"We'll keep watch tonight," Clint said. "They won't travel in the dark, but they may show up tomorrow, depending on how bad the injury was."

"This is just the kind of thing I do not need," Tesla said. "Once we reach the house, I will need to concentrate on my work."

"I'll make sure you're not interrupted," Clint said. "What about the other items you're having delivered. Where are they coming from?"

"Denver."

"That means they'll take the same route that we took today."

"So they will have to go through that same settlement," Tesla said. "They may have trouble with those men like we did."

"Maybe they won't be there," Clint said. "Or maybe they learned their lesson today."

"I am now thinking that it was a good idea for the President to send you to watch over me," Tesla said. "You proved that today."

"Well, let's just hope it doesn't go any further," Clint said. "I'll take the first watch. You get some sleep."

TWELVE

Roman Troy sat with his left hand around a shot glass of whiskey, and his right arm in a sling. His partners, Donnie Ward and Lefty Cole, sat across from him. They each had a glass of whiskey and were keeping quiet. Neither of them wanted to be the object of his anger, which was like a black cloud, ready to unleash a torrent.

"He's not gonna get away with this," Roman said for the hundredth time. He'd started at the doctor's office while the man put his arm in a sling, and he had repeated himself many times since then.

"We can get 'em when they come back this way, Roman," Donnie said.

Roman glared at him, and Donnie wished he hadn't spoken.

"When they come back? I ain't waitin' that long," Roman snapped.

"But—" Lefty started, then stopped himself, hoping Roman hadn't noticed.

"But what?" Roman demanded.

"Um, we don't know where they went."

"Well, we're gonna find out."

"How?"

"That fella with the ax handle, he went into Doyle's tent, right? If he bought somethin', maybe it's bein' delivered."

"Yeah, maybe," Donnie agreed.

"Well?" Roman said.

Donnie and Lefty stared at him.

"Go and find out," Roman said, crashing his left fist down on the table.

Both men jumped to their feet and ran out of the tent. "Naw," Doyle said. "He didn't buy nothin', and wasn't sellin' nothin'."

"Well then," Donnie said, "what was he doin' in here, Doyle?"

"Look, fellas," Doyle said, "I don't want no trouble. I just wanna sell my supplies."

"There ain't gonna be no trouble, Doyle," Lefty said. "Not if you tell us what you know."

"I don't know nothin'," Doyle said. "I tolja."

"He didn't come in here for no reason," Donnie said. "All he left with was that ax handle."

"You mean to tell us he came in here just for an ax handle?" Lefty said.

"Well, no but—"

Donnie reached out and grabbed the front of Doyle's shirt and said, "But what?"

"H-He did say somethin' about Gunnison."

"What? They were goin' to Gunnison?"

"I—I don't know," Doyle said. "H-He asked me how much farther it was to Gunnison."

Donnie looked at Lefty, released Doyle's shirt. The two men walked out.

"Gunnison?" Roman said.

"That's what Doyle said," Donnie answered.

"That they were goin' to Gunnison?"

"He said the fella with the ax handle asked how much farther it was to Gunnison."

"So they're headed that way," Roman said, "but we don't know if that's their last stop."

"I guess," Lefty said.

"We ain't guessin', Lefty," Roman said.

"Then what are we doin'?" Donnie asked.

"We're goin' to Gunnison," Roman said. He indicated his right arm. "Nobody gets away with this." He poured himself a whiskey and downed it. "Find Givens."

"Givens?" Lefty said, swallowing.

"What do we need him for?" Donnie asked doubtfully.

"What does anybody need Givens for," Roman said. "Ever?"

"Well . . ." Donnie said, "killin'."

"And I need him to back me up."

"You got us," Lefty said.

"Yeah," Roman said, moving his damaged arm, "you fellas backed me up real good against a man with an ax handle."

"H-He had a gun," Lefty said.

"And he looked like he knew how to use it."

"Yeah, right," Roman said, standing up. "That's why I need Givens. Find him for me."

Roman left the tent. Donnie and Lefty exchanged a look, then Donnie grabbed the bottle.

"If we're gonna talk to Givens, I need a drink."

Lefty pushed his glass over and said, "Yeah, me, too."

THIRTEEN

Clint was surprised at Gunnison as they rode in there two days later. It had a hotel, saloon, and jailhouse, all built of wood. Many of the other structures were tents, but they could smell the newly cut wood as they drove in. The town was growing.

As they drove farther, they saw a restaurant, and the general store.

"Let's get something to eat here," Clint suggested.

"Exactly what I was thinking," Tesla said.

They stopped the buckboard in front of the restaurant and went inside. Although they didn't sit near a window, Clint was still able to keep an eye on the buckboard while they ate.

Either the beef stew was delicious or they were simply sick of beans after three nights on the trail.

"Why don't we stay in the hotel and move on in the morning?" Tesla suggested.

"Do you know how much farther the house is?"

"Three, four hours," the scientist said. "Perhaps more."

"Then we'll camp on the trail. We still have some daylight left."

"But—"

"If we stay in the hotel, who's going to watch the buckboard?"

"We can be on watch, as we have been doing."

"Then one of us will be paying for a hotel bed he's not using."

"I can pay—"

"I'd much rather sleep on the trail, close to the buckboard."

Tesla opened his mouth to protest, then realized it would do no good.

"Very well," he said. "I suppose I will have to be satisfied with this beef stew."

"Once we get situated and I go hunting, I'll fix you a stew you won't believe."

"You will go out and shoot a cow?" Tesla asked.

"It won't be beef stew," Clint said. "It'll be venison."

"Venison?"

"Deer."

"I have never eaten a deer."

"You're in for a treat."

They finished their meal and went out to the buckboard. They stopped when they saw someone leaning against it.

"Who is that?" Tesla asked.

"I don't know."

"She's very attractive."

"Yes, she is."

She was tall, wearing men's jeans and a man's shirt beneath a fur jacket, and looked to be in her early thirties.

"Hello, gents," she said when they'd reached her.

"Hello," Tesla said.

"Can we help you with something?"

"Nothing in particular," she said. "I was just curious about two strangers in town."

"Are you curious about all strangers?" Clint asked. "Or just us."

"Pretty much all strangers in Gunnison," she said. "Ya see, that's my job." She pulled her jacket open to display the sheriff's badge pinned to her shirt.

"A lady sheriff?" Tesla blurted out.

"You see somethin' wrong with that?" she asked.

"Why no," Tesla said. "Unusual, perhaps, but not wrong."

"You got a problem with a female sheriff?" she asked Clint.

"Not at all," he said. "Providing you tell us your name."

"Sheriff Miranda Lawson," she said. "And you?"

"My name is Clint Adams," he said. "This is Nikola Tesla."

"Hello, Nick," she said. "I don't know who you are, but I sure know your friend here. What's the Gunsmith doin' in Gunnison?"

"Passing through."

"On the way to where?"

"There's a house a few hours north of here," Clint said. "That's where we're going."

"That's pretty high up," she said. "What are you gonna do there?"

"I am a scientist," Tesla said. "I'll be doing some experiments when we get there."

"What kind of experiments?"

"Electricity."

"Don't know much about that," Sheriff Lawson said. "I just wanted to make sure you weren't here to start any trouble."

"No trouble," Clint said.

"You boys like to have a drink before you go?" she asked. "A beer?"

"We just ate," Clint said. "We were about to be on our way."

"The saloon's right there," she said, pointing across the street. "You can see your buckboard from there."

"A beer?" Clint asked, looking at Tesla.

"A cold one?" Tesla asked the sheriff.

"Cold as ice," she said.

"That sounds good to me," Tesla said.

"Okay, then," Clint said, "let's go."

"Follow me," Miranda Lawson said.

FOURTEEN

In moments they were set up at the end of the bar with a beer each. She was right. Clint could see the buckboard through the window.

"To electricity," she said, lifting her mug.

They drank.

"How long have you been the law here?" Clint asked.

"About a week," she said. "Our last lawman was killed in the street. Folks left him lying there with the badge on. So I picked it up and pinned it on."

"You elected yourself sheriff?" Clint asked.

She shrugged.

"Nobody else wanted it, and nobody has since stepped up to take it."

"Any deputies?"

"Nope."

"Why don't you leave?" Tesla asked.

She looked at him.

"And go where? I've been here for years. Used to be a

whore, now I'm a sheriff. Where else could I go and do that?"

"You've got a point," Clint said.

"You fellas gonna be doin' your experimentin' long?" she asked.

"Ask my friend," Clint said.

"I'm not sure," Tesla said. "Could be weeks, or months."

"Well, either way you'll be coming back here for supplies," she said. "So we'll be seeing each other from time to time."

"I suppose so," Clint said.

She finished her beer and set the empty mug down on the bar.

"Stop in and see me then."

"Think you'll still be wearing that badge?" he asked.

She smiled and said, "I don't know. I guess you'll just have to wait and see."

She walked them back out to their buckboard.

"See? Safe and sound."

"That was not the case yesterday, at a settlement we passed through."

"You gotta watch where you stop around here," she said. "Lots of men around here think they take whatever their guns let them take."

"Well, Clint stopped them and didn't even use his gun, just an ax handle."

"Expecting more trouble?" she asked.

"You never know," Clint said. "Actually, you might be able to help us."

"With what?"

"We've got a wagon coming through with a delivery."

"What kind of delivery?"

"Some equipment," Tesla said, "that would be of no use to anyone but me."

"When's it comin'?"

Clint looked at Tesla.

"Should be here in the next couple of days."

"Well, I'll be on the lookout for it," she said. "Make sure it gets to you. In fact, maybe I'll ride along."

"Whatever you can do would be appreciated," Clint said, then added, "Sheriff."

"Miranda will do," she said. "I expect a hot meal if I ride up there."

"You'll get it."

"Clint has promised me some venison stew," Tesla added.

"That suits me."

"Then maybe we'll see you then," Clint said as he and Tesla climbed into their seat.

"Look forward to it," Miranda said.

Clint and Tesla left Gunnison, with Sheriff Miranda Lawson waving them away.

"She likes you," Tesla said.

"Think so?"

"Oh, yes," Tesla said. "She will not come up to the house just to see that my equipment is delivered."

"You an expert on women?"

"Not at all," Tesla said, "I am just telling you what I observed."

"Well, whatever the reason," Clint said, "maybe she'll see to it your equipment arrives. This trip wouldn't be worth much if it didn't."

"I wouldn't be able to do much at all," Tesla said.

"We should have talked about this in Denver," Clint said.

"We could have gotten a couple of guards to accompany the wagon. Who's delivering it?"

"A reputable firm," Tesla said, "I assure you."

"Well," Clint said, "I guess we'll find out just how reputable."

FIFTEEN

Roman didn't like that he had to go to Givens, but it was probably the only way he'd get the man to work with him.

Donnie and Lefty had found Givens in one of the whores' tents, and the man told them to send Roman over.

"I'll be here all day," he'd said, slapping the skinny whore on her naked rump.

Now Roman stepped up to the tent flap, heard the sounds from inside of two people grunting. He peered through the flap, saw Givens on top of a whore, hairy ass pumping away at her. She had her thin legs wrapped around him, and at that moment her eyes caught Roman's over Givens's shoulder, and she stuck her tongue out at him. He dropped the flap and stepped back quickly.

He decided to stand there and wait for the grunting and moaning to stop before trying to get the attention of Givens.

It took about fifteen more minutes before he heard the man roar. He kicked the dirt uncomfortably, thought about leaving, but then stepped up to the flap and shouted, "Hey, Givens!"

"That you, Roman?"

"Yeah, it's me."

"Come on in."

As he entered, he saw Givens pulling his long johns on over his wilting dick. The girl pulled her knees up to her chest and stared at Roman. Givens was a huge man, in more ways than one. Roman wondered why he always got such skinny whores.

"You wanna ride?" Givens asked, jerking a thumb at the whore. "I got her all ready for ya."

"No," Roman said, his stomach churning at the thought, "that's okay."

Givens turned to the whore and said, "Go get us a bottle of whiskey."

She stood up, showing a thick black bush between her legs as she pulled on a thin robe.

"I need some money," she said.

"Yeah, yeah." Givens dug some money from his pants, which were hanging on a pole. "Here. And don't take so long."

She pulled the robe tight around her and stepped out of the tent. Roman noticed she was barefoot, and didn't know how anybody could walk around like that.

"What's on yer mind?" Givens asked. "Heard you got yer arm broke."

"That's right," Roman said, "and that's what's on my mind."

"Lookin' to get back at the guy?"

"That's right."

"Who was it?"

"Just some fellas passin' through with a loaded buckboard."

"Loaded with what?"

Roman shrugged.

"We didn't get a chance to take a look," he said.

"So the three of ya got taken by these two fellas?" Givens asked.

"Just the one," Roman said. "The other one was no trouble."

"One man braced the three of you?"

"He surprised us."

"Good with a gun?"

Roman hesitated.

"He didn't use his gun, right?" Givens said. "Oh, yeah, Lefty said somethin' about an ax handle."

"That's right."

Givens chuckled. He looked around, found what he was looking for, a half-finished cigar. He picked it up, found a match, and lit it.

"Where is this fella?"

"Best we can tell, he left here to go to Gunnison."

"When did this happen?" Givens asked.

"A couple of days ago."

"Means they probably got to Gunnison today," Givens said. "More than likely they'll be comin' back this way eventually. Your arm might be healed by then. Ya don't wanna wait?"

"I want my revenge while this arm is still hurtin'," Roman said.

"So ya want me to go to Gunnison?"

"Not alone," Roman said. "We'll go with ya."

"Four of us, huh?" Givens said. "Ya think that's gonna be enough?"

"Should be," Roman said. "He ain't gonna surprise us again."

"Any way we can find out who he is first?"

Roman shrugged. "Don't know if anybody around here recognized him," he said. "Maybe in Gunnison."

"Yeah, Gunnison," Givens said. "Yeah, okay, maybe we'll find out there. And you'll pay my price, right?"

"Yeah, yeah, I'll pay your price."

"Okay, then get out."

"What?"

"That whore'll be back any minute with the bottle and I'm about ready to ride her again."

"Already?"

Givens grinned.

"Wanna stay and learn somethin'?"

"No, thanks," Roman said.

"I'll come by the saloon later and we'll make our plans," Givens said.

"Okay," Roman said, "but don't make me come here again, okay?"

"Why not?"

"I don't wanna ruin my dinner."

"Ya don't like skinny whores with a heavy bush between her legs?" Givens asked. "That's my favorite."

"Yeah, that's it," Roman said. "I don't wanna see the *girl* naked."

Roman left and passed the girl on the way. She was holding the bottle in one hand, and her robe with the other. She stuck her tongue out at him again.

SIXTEEN

Clint and Tesla rolled up to the house just before dark, and Tesla heaved a great sigh of relief.

"Thank God," he said. "I thought I was going to have to spend another night sleeping on the ground."

"We better see how much we can get unpacked before dark," Clint said, stepping down.

"Oh, there won't be much we can unpack ourselves," Tesla said.

"What do you mean?"

"These pieces of equipment are too heavy," Tesla said. "When they get here with the rest, they can unload everything for us."

"Well," Clint said, "we can take in the sundries, get some coffee going—if there's a working stove?"

"Supposed to be," Tesla said. "I shall be very upset if there isn't."

"Well, let's go inside and see what we've got," Clint suggested.

They approached the house, which looked to be solidly

built. It was one story, with a porch that ran the width of the house in front.

Clint tried the front door and found it open. Inside there was a large, empty front room, a kitchen off to one side, and in the back two bedrooms, which surprised Clint.

"Ah," Tesla said, "Just what I need. All this empty space."

Clint walked to the stove, inspected it, and said, "Doesn't look like we'll have any problems here either."

They checked the two bedrooms, found them to be about the same size, each with a single bed already made up with sheets and a blanket. Other than some dust all over everything, the house looked fine.

"This is even better than I had hoped," Tesla said.

"We'll need some lamps," Clint said. "I'll see if I can find any."

He found half a dozen lamps, a couple beneath the stove, and the rest hanging off the back of the house, where he found another porch. Farther back he could see an out-house.

Carrying all the lamps inside, he could feel that they had oil in them already.

"Whoever rented this house to you made sure you had everything."

"I told you," Tesla said. "I use reputable firms."

"Well," Clint said, "let's unpack what we can before it gets dark, and I'll use that stove to make us some supper."

"Venison stew?" Tesla asked hopefully.

"No," Clint said. "I have to go hunting for that. I'll do it tomorrow. Plenty of deer around here. I'll bag one tomorrow. Tonight, it's beans and bacon."

They carried in what they could, mostly food, coffee, blankets, Clint's bag and rifle, and Tesla's bag with his personal belongings. Clint saw some of Tesla's equipment on the buckboard, saw that a lot of it was made of metal.

"What are those?" he asked, pointing.

"Electrodes."

"I don't know what those are," Clint said.

"I'll show you, when I get everything ready."

When they got what they could inside, Clint went out and took care of the team. There was a lean-to behind the house that he pressed into service as a livery. He then collected wood for the stove. He got it lit and started a pot of coffee, then set about to make the bacon and beans. Before long the house smelled of food and coffee, and was warm. They were able to remove their jackets.

Tesla sat at the table with a cup of coffee and watched Clint cook.

"You can do many things I cannot," Tesla said.

"Like what? Shoot a gun?"

"More than that," he replied. "Cook, hunt, the way you stood up to those three men with an ax handle. You could have used your gun and you chose not to."

"A gun is not always the way," Clint said.

He filled two metal plates with beans and bacon, carried them to the table. He set one down in front of Tesla, then sat across from him with his own plate and coffee.

"When will you start doing . . . whatever it is you're going to do?" Clint asked.

"I need the rest of my equipment. When it arrives, there will be enough men to carry everything in. Then I can get started."

Clint poured out two more cups of coffee, scraped the rest of the bacon and beans into their plates.

"I'll get an early start in the morning," he said.

"Hunting?"

"Yes."

"May I come with you? I've never hunted before."

"But you've fired a rifle?"

"Yes, but not at anything living. I have nothing else to do until all my equipment is here and unloaded."

"Okay," Clint said. "We'll go hunting at first light. Meanwhile, we'll continue to keep watch. I'll take the first, and wake you in four hours."

"It will be a pleasure to sleep in a bed tonight."

SEVENTEEN

In the morning Clint awoke and smelled coffee. He rolled out of bed. He'd had a good four hours on a mattress that had been better than half the hotels he'd stayed in over the years.

When he came out of the room, Tesla was standing by the stove, watching the coffeepot. He turned his head and saw Clint.

"Good morning."

"Mornin'," Clint said.

"I would have started breakfast, but I am much better at cooking over an open fire."

"That's okay," Clint said. "I'll make some bacon. Too bad we didn't get some eggs while we were in Gunnison."

"That would have been nice."

"I'll probably have to go back there for supplies at some point," Clint said. "I'll see if I can get some."

"How long can we last on the supplies we have?" Tesla asked.

"A couple of weeks."

"Well, we can worry about it then," he said, "unless we find some chickens wandering about."

"Not likely," Clint said. "Any chicken found its way out here would get devoured by a big cat."

"Big cat?"

"Mountain lion," Clint said. "These mountains belong to them. If we want a deer today, we'll have to beat a mountain lion to it."

"Mountain lions?" Tesla asked. "Seriously?"

"Oh yeah," Clint said. "They are the top hunters up here."

Tesla stared at Clint as the coffee started to boil over. Clint grabbed the pot and took it off the stove.

"Get the cups and pour," Clint said. "I'll put on the bacon."

He cut strips of bacon and put them in a frying pan. Before long the house was filled with the scent of sizzling bacon.

They finished their breakfast and stepped outside. It was cold, but not oppressively so. They each held their rifles, and Clint was wearing his modified Colt.

"What do we do now?" Tesla asked.

"We walk," Clint said. "Until we see some sign of a deer—or a mountain lion."

"You keep talking about mountain lions," Tesla said. "Are you trying to frighten me?"

"Not at all," Clint said. "I just want you to realize what we have to deal with up here."

"So what do we do if we come upon one?" Tesla asked. "A mountain lion, I mean."

"We leave it alone as long as it leaves us alone."

"And if it doesn't leave us alone?"

"Then we kill it before it kills us," Clint said. "Let's start walking."

"So if I could invent a gun that would fire electricity," Tesla was saying half an hour later, "what would you think of that?"

"What good would it do?" Clint asked.

"Well . . . it would fire electricity instead of lead," Tesla said.

"I understand that," Clint said. "My question is . . . why? What for?"

"It would be better than bullets," Tesla said.

"I'm afraid I'd have to see that to believe it," Clint said. "Could I hit a deer at three hundred yards with your gun?"

"Can you do that now?"

"Yes."

Tesla looked surprised.

"Three hundred yards?"

"Yes."

He frowned, obviously unhappy.

"I don't know if I could sustain an electrical charge over that distance."

"Then I guess you still have some work to do."

"Well, when I have the time—"

"Shh," Clint said, holding up his hand.

Tesla obeyed, fell silent.

Clint pointed straight ahead of them.

"I don't see anything," Tesla whispered.

"Tracks," Clint said.

"What kind?"

"Deer, maybe."

"M-Mountain lion?"

"No," Clint said, "not yet. Look."

He pointed to the ground, but Tesla still didn't see anything.

"I will just follow you," he said, "while you follow the tracks."

"All right."

EIGHTEEN

Roman, Donnie, and Lefty rode into Gunnison with Givens trailing them. Roman held the reins in his left hand, kept his right tight to his body, still in a sling.

Abruptly, Givens rode up to join Roman.

"We know who the law is hereabouts?" he asked.

"Got no law to speak of," Roman said. "Their last lawman got gunned down in the street, and folks just left him there for the longest time, way I heard it."

"I heard some whore picked up his badge and pinned it on," Lefty said.

They all looked at him.

"Hey," he said, shrugging, "that's what I heard."

"A whore turned sheriff," Givens said. "Now that sounds interestin'. Maybe she knows somethin'."

"I ain't about to talk to the law, even if it is a whore," Roman said.

"I'll go and talk to her," Givens volunteered.

"Fine," Roman said. "We'll wait for you at the saloon."

They split up there.

Givens dismounted in front of the sheriff's office, which had a boarded-up window in front. He wondered if the office was even in use. Maybe the female sheriff was still working out of a whorehouse.

He walked to the front door and opened it. There was a woman with long hair seated at the desk. She looked up as he entered, and her eyes widened when she saw him.

"Can I help you?" she asked, looking him up and down. Givens knew his size brought him to the attention of both men and women, for different reasons. She looked interested in what she was seeing.

"Yeah, I just rode into town," he said. "I'm lookin' for a couple of men and thought the sheriff would be able to help me."

"Well, I'm Sheriff Lawson," she said.

"Yeah, I heard there was a woman sheriff here in Gunnison," he said. "But I didn't hear you were beautiful."

"Yeah, well," she said, "smooth talk'll only get you so far. What was it you wanted? Information on two men you're lookin' for?"

"That's right."

"What's their names?"

"I don't know their names," he said, "but they're drivin' a buckboard with a heavy load."

"Ah . . ."

"Does that mean you saw them?"

"What do you want with them?"

"Why's that matter?"

"I'm just curious."

"A woman's curiosity, or a lawman's?"

"Are lawmen usually curious?" she asked. "Let's say the female part of me and the law part of me want to know if you plan on killing these men."

Suddenly, Givens wasn't so friendly. He started to get to his feet, saying, "Now listen, girlie," when he suddenly found himself looking down the barrel of a Peacemaker. She cocked the hammer, and they both remained silent for a few moments.

Then he sat back down.

"Okay," he said, "okay. Calm down."

"I'm calm," she said. "But I won't be spoken to or treated rudely. Do you understand?"

"Yes, I do."

"Now ask me your question again."

"Have you seen two men with an overloaded buckboard go through here in the past few days?"

"No," she lied. "Next question."

NINETEEN

Clint followed the trail until it crossed with that of a mountain lion.

"Stop."

"What?" Tesla asked.

"There." Clint pointed to the ground.

The track was clear enough for even Tesla to see. A large paw track.

"My God," he said. "That's huge."

"Yeah," Clint said, looking around, "it's pretty big."

"What's it—where's it going?"

"It's following our deer."

"Oh," Tesla said. "Well, can't we find another deer? Why do we have to go after the same one?"

"You want venison stew, don't you?" Clint asked.

"Not if it means I have to fight a mountain lion for it."

Clint laughed.

"Don't worry," he said, "I won't make you fight a mountain lion."

"Good."

"Shoot one, maybe," Clint said, "but not fight one."

Givens found the other three men at the saloon, each holding a beer, or leaning over it on the bar.

"Beer," he said to the bartender.

"What did the whore sheriff have to say?" Roman asked.

"Nothin'," Givens replied. "Says she didn't see our guys."

"You believe her?"

"No."

"Why didn't you make her tell you the truth?"

Givens took his beer and sipped it, then looked at Roman.

"Why don't *you* go over and make her tell you?"

Roman frowned at Givens, then turned his head.

"After this we'll go over and talk to some of the merchants. Somebody must know somethin'," Givens said. "We'll split up and find out."

"Maybe I will go and see the sheriff," Roman said.

"Yeah," Givens said, "maybe."

About an hour later Clint and Tesla stopped again.

"What is it?"

"Let's just sit here awhile."

"I won't complain about that."

They sat down on some rocks.

"Do you think a deer will come walking by?" the scientist asked.

"Actually," Clint said, "one might. There are a lot of tracks here."

"How will we get it back to the house?" Tesla asked. "Aren't they heavy?"

"If we wanted the whole animal, I'd sling it over my

shoulders and carry it back," Clint said. "But I'll butcher it out here. We'll take some of the best cuts and leave the rest for the cat."

"Do you think the cat will appreciate the gesture?"

"Not at all," Clint said. "He'll probably eat his fill, and then follow us to get the rest."

"Will you kill him?"

"Not unless I have to," Clint said. "He's just trying to survive."

"Like the rest of us?"

"Yes."

"Well," Tesla said, "maybe I can't carry an entire deer carcass on my shoulders, but I'm sure I can carry some meat."

"Okay," Clint said. "We'll sit here awhile and see what happens. In a little while we'll start moving again."

"How long will we stay out here?" Tesla asked.

"We'll be back at the house before dark," Clint said. "Guaranteed."

"Very well."

Givens, Roman, Lefty, and Donnie left the saloon.

"They must have had somethin' to eat," Givens said. "Somebody check the restaurants. Can't be that many."

"I'll do it," Donnie said.

"Somebody else check the general store."

"Me," Lefty said.

"I'll go back inside and talk to the bartender," Givens said. "Roman, you want to talk to the sheriff?"

"We'll meet back here in an hour," Roman said. "Somebody better find out something."

Givens watched the three of them walk away, then turned and went back into the saloon.

*   *   *

"See it?" Clint asked twenty minutes later. "There, straight on."

"I do," Tesla whispered.

There was a deer about a hundred yards off, just standing and looking around. It was a young male, with just stubs where his antlers would soon be.

"You want to take a shot?" Clint asked.

"No," Tesla said. "If I miss, we will lose him. You shoot."

"Okay," Clint said. "You can try next time."

Clint shouldered his rifle and fired one shot, dropping the animal cleanly.

Tesla started forward, but Clint held his arm out to block him.

"Slowly," he said. "That lion is still around."

Tesla nodded, didn't move until Clint did.

A half a mile away, a mountain lion lifted its head at the sound of the shot and listened intently. Then it sniffed the air.

And then it moved.

TWENTY

Roman had a sneaking suspicion that Givens had never left the saloon.

The big man was halfway through a beer when he saw Roman. He turned to the bartender and said, "Bring a cold one."

Roman joined him at the bar as the bartender put the beer down.

"So?" Givens asked. "Any news?"

"No," Roman said, "I didn't find any merchants who saw them."

"Or they won't say," Givens said. "Folks like to mind their own business."

"We'll have to see what Donnie and Lefty come up with."

"It won't matter," Givens said. "The barkeep here told me he saw the sheriff in here with two strangers. He thinks they may be the ones we're lookin' for."

"How's he know?"

"He saw a heavily loaded buckboard outside."

"Does he know where they went?"

"No, but maybe the sheriff does."

"That whore?"

"She's wearin' a badge," Givens pointed out. "Why don't we wait for Donnie and Lefty to get back and then we'll ask 'er?"

Sheriff Miranda Lawson saddled her horse quickly, keeping an eye out so no one could come up behind her. The word she'd gotten was that the man she'd spoken to and three friends were all looking for Clint Adams and his friend, Tesla. Whatever the reason was for that, it couldn't be good. She also knew they'd find out that she was in the saloon with both men, so she thought it was a good time to get out of town.

She mounted up and rode out of the livery. She figured she could kill two birds with one stone by leaving town and riding to warn Clint Adams. She had a general idea where the house was that he and Tesla were renting. He may have been the Gunsmith, but he still needed some warning that four gunmen were looking for him.

The heavily laden buckboard rode into Gunnison, noisily announcing its arrival. There were two burly men on the seat, looking worn out from the drive from Denver.

Givens and Roman had just stepped out of the saloon as the buckboard came down the street, and the big man put his hand on Roman's chest to stop him.

"Where do you suppose they're goin'?" he asked.

"Beats me. Why?"

"Well, the two fellers we're lookin' for had a loaded buckboard."

"So?"

"So suppose this load is also theirs?" Givens asked. "All we'd have to do is follow it."

"So how do we find out?"

"Easy," Givens said. "We ask 'em."

"We gotta stop for some food and beer," Joe Scott said.

"I can go ya one better," Les Willard said. "Let's spend the night. I don't wanna sleep on the trail again, and we should be able to get this load delivered tomorrow."

"Ya think?"

"That's the plan," Willard said.

"Suits me."

"Let's find someplace to put up this load."

Once Givens realized the two men were going to stay, he suggested that he and Roman just wait in the saloon. Eventually, Lefty and Roman showed up, and Givens and Roman told them what was going on.

"So we're just gonna wait here?" Donnie asked.

"That's right," Givens said. "Those two are gonna want a drink eventually."

"Suits me," Lefty said.

"And I got another idea," Givens said to Roman.

"What?"

"I'm the only one ain't been seen by those two you tangled with," Givens said.

"So?"

"So maybe these two would like some help from a big man like me unloading that buckboard when they get where they're goin'."

Roman brightened.

"That's a good idea."

"Yeah," Givens said. "I thought so. Why don't you and the boys go and see what you can find out from the sheriff? There's no point in letting them know I'm with you. When they get here, I'll try and get myself a job."

TWENTY-ONE

The smell of Clint's venison stew filled the house. Tesla was sitting at the table, reading some books. Clint cut up some onions and potatoes he had bought in Denver and added them to the stew, then mixed it.

The rest of the meat he had butchered was hanging off the back wall of the house, in the cold, up high where animals could not reach it. He was sure the big cat was feasting on the remains of the carcass Clint had left behind for him, but when he was finished, he'd come looking for more.

If they were going to be staying in this house for a long period of time, the day would come when he'd have to face the cat.

When the stew was ready, he poured it into two bowls and carried them to the table. He went back to the stove and returned with coffee cups, then sat opposite Tesla. The scientist put his books aside and spooned some of the stew into his mouth.

"By God!" he exclaimed. "I don't think I've ever tasted anything better."

"Part of the reason for that is that we hunted it ourselves," Clint said. "No meat ever tastes as good."

"I can see that." He had another bite, with potato and onion. "You're quite a cook, Clint. I was assuming my meals would be meager while I was here. I'll have to thank the President."

"There's plenty left," Clint said. "You can have more, we can heat it later, or tomorrow for lunch."

"And the rest of the meat?"

"Hung up high, where the big cat can't get to it—hopefully."

"What about other animals?"

"There are plenty," Clint said. "Other predators. But he's the one we have to worry about."

"Will he come at night? Try to get into the house?"

"No," Clint said, "he'll stay outside. But come at night? He might."

"But we will be on the lookout for men," Tesla said. "Will we not then be on the lookout for the cat?"

"We will," Clint said. "On the other hand, if there are men who are coming here to kill you, maybe the cat will take care of them for us. We'll have to wait and see."

Clint decided to start unloading the buckboard now, and not wait for the rest of Tesla's equipment to show up with a couple of men to help him.

"There must be something you have that we can bring in ourselves now," Clint said.

"It's all pretty heavy," Tesla said.

He was right. Apart from some antennae that were easy to carry, the rest of it was metal and heavy.

Tesla was apparently able to sit in one place for long periods of time and think about his experiments. Although Clint could sit comfortably in the evening and read, during the day he grew antsy.

While Tesla sat inside and went through his books, Clint went out back to check on the meat. He'd hung it high. Judging by the claw marks on the back of the house, some kind of animal had tried to climb up the wall and get it. He doubted it was the big cat. That animal probably could have leaped that high if it really wanted to.

He walked around the entire house, checking for any sign of the big cat. There were other tracks, smaller animals like badgers, prairie dogs, mule deer, and the like. No sign, though, that the big one had come around—yet.

He went around to the front of the house and wished they had brought some wooden chairs with them. He made do by sitting down on the edge of the porch.

He spent a couple of hours there, just watching, until it was time to make supper.

Tesla agreed that heated venison stew would make a fine meal.

"What were you doing outside today?" Tesla asked as they ate.

"Staying out of your way," Clint said.

"Did you see anything?"

"If you mean the cat, no. I've seen other tracks, but not his."

"That is good, right?"

"So far."

"Well, I can use your help with something."

"What would that be?"

"Since we brought the antennae in," Tesla said, "I'd like to erect them on the roof. Can you help me with that?"

"Sure," Clint said. "We'll still have some daylight after we finish eating. Let's do it then. Do you want to be on the roof, or on the ground?"

TWENTY-TWO

When Roman, Lefty, and Donnie got back to the saloon, Givens was at the bar, alone.

"Where are your new friends?" Roman asked.

"Joe and Les went to get somethin' to eat."

"So you got their names?"

"Well, of course," Givens said. "If I'm gonna help them unload their wagon, we should know each other's names, right?"

"So they hired you?"

"In a minute."

"Good. Did they tell you the names of the other two?" Roman asked.

"Just one," Givens said. "Nikola Tesla."

"Nikola?" Donnie said. "What the hell kinda name is that?"

"Foreign," Givens said. "They said the guy was foreign."

"Well, the one with the ax handle, he ain't foreign," Lefty said. "I'd still like to know who he is."

"What happened with the sheriff?" Givens asked.

"Nothin'," Roman said.

"She ain't around," Lefty said. "I think maybe you scared her off."

"It don't matter," Givens said. "Joe and Les are gonna take us right to Mr. Tesla and his friend."

"When?" Roman asked.

"First thing in the mornin'."

"So we got all night?" Donnie asked.

"All night," Givens said.

"Good," he said. "Lookin' for that sheriff started me thinking about whores."

"Me, too," Lefty said.

"Well, go ahead," Roman said. "Have all the whores you can afford. Just meet me in front of the livery first thing in the morning."

"Just don't show yerselves until me and my new friends head out," Givens said.

"You got it," Lefty said, and he and Donnie headed out the door.

"What're you gonna do, Givens?" Roman asked.

"Eat somethin', and then come right back here. Why? You thinkin' about whores, too?"

"Well . . ."

TWENTY-THREE

Miranda camped on the trail that night, spent most of the night awake. She felt someone—something—in the dark, watching her. Her horse was uneasy, and several times she had to calm it so it would not pull free of its restraint. If it had been the men from Gunnison, they would surely have taken her. More likely it was an animal, hungry, but frightened of the fire. She dozed, but came awake often enough to keep the fire going.

At first light she saddled up, broke camp, but before mounting up, she walked the perimeter of the camp and found the tracks. They were huge. Some kind of big cat. Now she knew why her horse had been so uneasy. She was going to have to be careful the rest of the day.

She mounted up and began to ride.

Roman, Donnie, and Lefty spent the evening with whores, and then Roman stayed the entire night with his.

He rolled over in the morning and stared at the girl next to him. She had a fleshy body, but then she had to be close to forty. There wasn't much of a choice when it came right down to it, but he liked women with pale skin and dark hair, so the fact that she was a little meaty was something he overlooked. In the end he was fortunate, because she was very experienced and did things with him that he usually had to pay extra for.

As he watched, she rolled over onto her back. Her big breasts flopped to the right and left, but he didn't mind. Her skin was very white, which made her big, brown nipples look even darker. He leaned over and took one nipple into his mouth, then the other. She moaned, reached to cup his head to her breast.

She moaned as he slid his hand between her legs, found her hairy pussy already wet. Suddenly, his cock was rock hard. He slid a leg over her, mounted, and slid his cock into her. She was hot and ready, wrapped her legs around his waist, and held on while he fucked her, slamming in and out of her mindlessly . . .

Givens met his new friends, Joe and Les, at the livery. They had the buckboard team already hooked up as he strode up.

"Just let me saddle my horse and I'll be right with ya," he called.

They waved and Joe said, "No hurry."

Givens saddled his horse, wondering if Roman and the others were watching. He didn't want them to be too far behind the buckboard when they left.

He walked his horse out and mounted up.

"Ready?" he asked.

"Let's go," Les said, and snapped the reins at the team.

Givens risked a look behind him, didn't see anyone. Those assholes better not have fallen so far into their whores that they overslept!

* * *

Roman got to the livery in time to see the buckboard pull away. He hurriedly saddled his horse, was ready to go by the time Donnie and Lefty got there.

"Get your asses saddled up," he shouted. "They left ten minutes ago."

"Yeah, yeah," Lefty said, hung over.

Donnie silently saddled his horse. He just wanted to get going.

They walked their horses outside and mounted up.

"We got some easy tracks to follow," Roman said. "I'll take the lead."

The other two didn't care who had the lead. They were going to doze in their saddles anyway.

TWENTY-FOUR

Clint prepared a batch of flapjacks and some bacon for breakfast.

"I swear before the rest of my equipment arrives, I will gain twenty pounds," Tesla said.

"We can move on to smaller meals, then," Clint said.

"No, no," Tesla said, "I'm not complaining, just making an observation."

Clint was about to reply when he heard the sound of a horse approaching.

"What is it?" Tesla asked.

"Someone's approaching."

"The cat?" Tesla looked nervous.

"No," Clint said, "someone on horseback." He stood up. "Wait here."

Clint rode, walked to the front window, and looked out. He saw a rider sitting tall in the saddle, riding up to the house. He had strapped his gun belt on earlier that morning, when he first dressed, so he walked to the door, opened it, and stepped out.

As the rider drew closer, he recognized her.

"Sheriff Lawson," he greeted. "What brings you all this way?"

"I have something to tell you," she said. "Is that bacon I smell?"

"And flapjacks. Step down and join us, if you've nowhere else to go."

"This was my destination," she said.

"Then come inside. I'll set you up with a meal and then see to your horse."

"Thank you."

She tied off her horse and followed him inside. Tesla stood as she entered.

"Sheriff," he said. "What a pleasant surprise."

"Mr. Tesla," she said.

"The sheriff has come to join us for breakfast," Clint said. "Sit, please, Sheriff."

"Miranda," she said. "Please call me Miranda."

"Flapjacks and bacon, Miranda?" Clint asked.

"And coffee, please."

"Coming up."

He quickly whipped up a stack of cakes and strips of bacon and set them before her.

"I'll see to your horse if you're going to stay awhile."

"Maybe I should first tell you why I've come," she offered.

"All right." Clint poured himself some more coffee and sat at the table with Tesla and Miranda. "What's on your mind?"

She told him.

"Four men?" Clint asked when she was done. "Not three?"

"Four," she asked. "The one who came to see me was a big brute."

"He didn't hurt you?"

"He looked down the barrel of my gun," she said.

"Good for you," Tesla said.

"But I thought it was wise for me to leave town," she added. "And I figured I might as well warn you."

"We appreciate it," Clint said. "I'll see to your horse now, and arrange a room for you."

"I don't want to put you out. If you have a barn—"

"You'll take my room," he said. "I can bunk out here with my bedroll."

"A bed," she said, "and a wonderful breakfast. What more could a girl ask for?"

Clint left to take care of her horse.

"So those men are looking for us?" Tesla asked.

"Yes."

"Well," he said, "if they find us, I'm sure Clint can take care of them."

"Four against one?" she asked.

"Well . . . that is supposed to be what he does, isn't it?"

"I guess so," she said.

"More coffee?" he asked.

She smiled and said, "Please."

TWENTY-FIVE

Clint unsaddled Miranda's roan, rubbed it down, and gave it some of the feed he'd bought in Denver for the team—something else Tesla had forgotten to buy.

When he reentered the house, Miranda was standing at the stove. He put her rifle and saddlebags down by the door.

"The coffeepot went dry," she said. "I made some more."

"Thank you."

"I made it strong, since the cup you gave me would have removed paint."

"That's the way I like it," Clint said.

"So do I."

"Does anyone want the last piece of bacon?" Tesla asked.

"No," Clint said.

"You have it," Miranda said.

Tesla plucked it from the plate and popped it into his mouth.

They had more coffee and then Miranda insisted on cleaning the plates and cups. Tesla went to his room to read his books. Clint sat at the table and watched her, drinking another cup of coffee.

"Did you camp on the trail last night?" he asked.

"I did."

"You didn't happen to run into a big cat, did you?"

She turned and looked at him.

"I felt something looking at me from the dark. In the morning I saw the tracks. Have you seen it?"

"No," he said. "We were hunting and crossed its trail. Haven't seen it, but it's a big one judging by the tracks."

"What were you hunting?"

"Deer."

"Bad one?"

"A young buck. Left most of it for the cat."

"He won't thank you."

"I know."

"What'd you make?"

"Venison stew."

"Any left?"

He smiled.

"I can make more," he said. "Mr. Tesla has acquired a taste for it."

"Good," she said. "I acquired a taste for it a long time ago."

She came and sat at the table with him. She brought the pot and emptied it into his cup.

"How long do you intend to stay with us?" he asked.

"I don't know. I guess if I stay here, I'll have to face those four, and if I go back, I'll have to face them."

"Better you stay here, then," Clint said. "Face them with me, if the time comes."

"As you say," she said. "Meanwhile, maybe I can help."

"Tesla's equipment is heavy," Clint said. "We're waiting for two more men to arrive with still another buckboard load, and then we'll all unload it."

"Another buckboard?" she said. "From Denver?"

"Yes."

"It'll have to go through Gunnison, like you did," she said.

"That's right."

"Then those four men . . ."

"Will probably take it."

"Yes."

"But what would they do with all that equipment?" he asked. "They wouldn't even know what it was for. No, something else is more likely."

"Like what?"

"Like they would follow it."

"Follow it here," she said.

"Yes."

"So I'm right," she said. "We'll have to face them."

"Probably, and yet—"

"And yet what?"

And yet it wasn't those four men he had been hired to protect Tesla from. It was others, unknown others rumored to want him dead.

"Nothing," he said. "We'll have to set some watches. You and me."

"Not Mr. Tesla?"

"He has other work that he came here to do," Clint said. "Besides, he wouldn't see what you and I will see. No, it'll just be you and me."

"Watch from where?"

"We'll need to see them before they get here," he said.

"They'll be coming from Denver. We'll have to find ourselves a good point to watch from."

"Let's do it, then," she said.

They both stood up.

"I'll tell Tesla we're going out," he said.

TWENTY-SIX

Clint and Miranda walked away from the house, back in the direction she had come. No one had come up to that house in a long time prior to Clint and Tesla's arrival. There was a road, but it was partially overgrown with grass. Still visible, though.

"Once they spot this road, they'll follow it up," Clint said.

"So we need to find a place to watch this road from, right?"

"Right. But one of us will always have to be back at the house, as well."

"Why?" she asked. "Isn't the danger coming from here?"

"The danger we know of," he said.

"You mean, there's more?" she asked. "Do you mean the cat?"

"Look," he said, "I'm here to keep an eye on Tesla while he does some experiments. There's a rumor that someone might try to hurt him, or kill him."

"So you're his bodyguard?"

"That's right."

"Who's payin' you?"

"I can't say."

Miranda shrugged.

"Doesn't matter much to me," she said. "Okay, so when one of us is out here, the other one is back at the house with Mr. Tesla."

"Right. So let's find our spot."

They found a good vantage point where they'd be hidden by a stand of trees. They were able to see down the road a few hundred yards.

"If that buckboard is loaded the way you say," she commented, "we'll be able to hear it comin'."

"That's true."

"Do you want me to take the first watch?" she asked.

"Okay," he said, "but don't expect that they'll actually be with the buckboard. They might be following it, or they could be coming on their own."

"I'll be ready for anythin'," she promised.

"I'll relieve you in four hours," he promised.

"That's fine," she said. "I'll sit here and enjoy the fresh air."

"Just be on the lookout for predators," he said, "two legged and four."

Clint walked back to the house. When he entered, Tesla was sitting at the table, and it was covered with books.

"Where is our lovely sheriff?" he asked.

"She on lookout," he said. "I'll relieve her in four hours."

"And me?"

"You're here to do your business," Clint said. "She and I will split the watch."

Clint looked down at the sheriff's saddlebags, then picked

them up and set them on a chair. He started to go through them.

"Why are you doing that?" Tesla asked.

"Because all we know about her is what she's told us," Clint said.

"You mean, you don't trust her?"

"Not at all."

"Then why did you put her on watch?"

"So that she doesn't know I don't trust her."

"But . . . those men could arrive, and we wouldn't know," Tesla said. "I mean, if she's working with them, she wouldn't warn us."

"That's right." Clint put her saddlebags back on the floor, satisfied there was nothing in them worth seeing—an extra shirt, some bullets, no letters to identify her. "That's why, while she's on watch, I'll be watching her—at least, in the beginning."

He turned and opened the door.

"Keep your gun handy, just in case," he advised.

"I shall keep it by my side."

He was already engrossed in his books when Clint went out the door.

Miranda was relaxed as she sat with her rifle across her knees. She knew Clint Adams didn't have to trust her right away. It might take time, but at least she wasn't in Gunnison, having to face four gunmen by herself. As a whore, she had always been confident that she could handle men, even more than one at a time. But as a sheriff, she had very little experience. Better to have a man like the Gunsmith backing her up when it came time to face more than one man with a gun.

TWENTY-SEVEN

Clint found a good vantage point from which he could watch both the road and Sheriff Miranda, and also keep a wary eye out for a mountain lion, or rumored killers.

He should have checked Miranda's bona fides when they were in Gunnison, but he never expected her to show up at the house. He supposed she could have been planted in Gunnison to wait for them, and then make their acquaintance, but he doubted she'd go through all the trouble of wearing the badge. After all, a badge made you a target, no matter what town you were in, and why do that if she was waiting for them to appear?

He settled down to watch the watcher.

The predator could see everything from his vantage point. The woman watching the road, the man watching the woman. The only one he couldn't see was the man still inside the house.

The predator was in no hurry, however. He settled down into a relaxed pose and was content to wait.

Clint relieved Miranda after four hours, told her to go back to the house. He followed her, positioned himself outside, peering in a window. If she was there to kill Tesla, this was her chance, but instead she simply poured herself a cup of coffee and sat down at the table with the scientist, who didn't seem to mind the interruption.

Clint watched as the two had a conversation. He noticed that Miranda did not have her rifle, probably left it by the door, and she had also removed her gun belt, probably hanging on the wall by the door. If she wanted to kill Nikola Tesla, she was going to have to reach across the table and strangle him.

Clint watched just a little while longer, then decided his initial feeling about Miranda was right. She was who she said she was, a whore turned sheriff who found herself with more than she could handle in Gunnison. She had come not only to warn them, but to give herself a good chance to survive if she had to face four gunmen.

Clint turned and walked back to keep an eye on the road.

As it started to get dark, he returned to the house. He doubted anybody in a buckboard would try traveling up the mountain in the dark, even if they were on a well-traveled road.

When he entered, Tesla was, as usual, engrossed in his books. Miranda was sitting across the table from him, cleaning her pistol.

"Time for supper?" she asked.

"Time to cook it," Clint said. "You two just remain as you are. I can work around you."

Tesla looked up, as if he'd suddenly realized Clint was there, and said, "Huh?"

"Relax, Nikola," Miranda said. "Just keep readin' your books."

She got up and joined Clint at the stove.

"I'm bored. Put me to work?"

He turned and looked at her.

"Can you peel potatoes?"

"Like an expert."

"Onions?"

"If you don't mind the crying," she said.

"Okay," Clint said. "You can help."

TWENTY-EIGHT

Tesla cleared his books off the table for supper. Miranda set the table, then helped Clint carry the food and coffee.

"Wow," she said after her first bite.

"That's what I said," Tesla said. "It's wonderful, isn't it?"

"Amazing," she said. She looked at Clint. "Where did you learn to cook?"

"On the trail."

"That's over an open fire," she said. "Now you're usin' a stove."

"I graduated."

"You sure you didn't learn from a woman?"

"Sorry," Clint said. "No woman."

"Wife? Mother?"

"Neither."

"You've been single all these years?"

"Yes."

"Then I guess you're one of those men."

"Which men?"

"The ones I used to meet in my other job."

"Sorry," he said, shaking his head. "No whores."

"What's wrong with whores?" she demanded.

"Nothing," he said. "I just don't like to pay a woman to be with me."

She stared at him for a few moments, then said, "No, I guess you don't have to, do ya?"

Tesla ate in earnest, hardly listening to their conversation.

"Well," she said, "you'll make some woman a fine husband someday."

"Not me," he said. "I'm not really the marrying kind. No, I'll die single."

"Well, if you know that, do you know how you'll die?" she asked.

"In the saddle," Clint said, "probably at the end of a bullet."

"You expect that?"

"Given the kind of life I lead, yeah," Clint said. "I'd actually prefer it to a lot of other ways a man could die."

"Like what?" Tesla asked, suddenly interested.

"Like wasting away in a bed, the way Doc Holliday did," Clint said. "Like being shot from behind, like Wild Bill Hickok. I won't mind being shot to death, as long as it comes from the front. But don't get me wrong. I don't want to have it happen for a long time yet."

Tesla was going to say something else, but he was interrupted by the sound of a scream from outside.

"The horses," Clint said.

He bolted from the table to the door and outside. He circled the house and ran toward the makeshift stable. As he got there, he saw that one of the three horses was down.

As he reached it, he could smell the blood. The horse that was down was one of the team, not Miranda's roan.

He heard footsteps from behind, turned, and saw Miranda and Tesla running toward him, both carrying rifles.

"What was it?" Miranda asked.

"Was it the cat?"

"Yeah, it was," Clint said. He looked down at the paw prints that surrounded the lean-to. The cat had circled the animals for a while before striking. The horses must have been reacting, must have been nervous, but the people in the house had been so involved in their supper and conversation that they hadn't heard anything until it was too late.

The mountain lion had literally ripped a chunk out of the horse's neck, cutting its scream off. The cat hadn't had time to do much else, but it must have carried a hunk away with it to feed on.

"That poor animal," Tesla said. "I thought the cat wouldn't come in the dark?"

"It must have been hungry enough to do it," Clint said. "We're going to have to watch the other two horses from now on."

"What do we do with this one?" Tesla asked.

"We'll have to drag it away," Clint said. "When we get it away from the house, maybe the cat will gorge itself on the carcass, and be satisfied for a while."

"But . . . how do you move it?" Tesla asked.

"We'll get some ropes, hook them up to the other horses, and drag it away. And we better get started before it's totally dark. If that cat's willing to hunt in the dark, there's no telling where it is."

"Where are the ropes?" Miranda asked.

"On the buckboard, holding the equipment in place beneath the tarp. We just have to untie it."

"Let's get to it, then," she said. "I think Mr. Tesla should stand by us with his rifle."

"Suits me," Clint said. "Nikola?"

"Yes, all right," Tesla said nervously. "I—I will watch your backs."

"Right now," Clint said, "watch these other two horses while we get the ropes."

"Yes, right."

As Clint and Miranda walked away, Tesla anxiously gripped and regripped his rifle.

The predator looked on, watched the two men and woman work on moving the carcass of the horse. He could have taken action then, but it was dark, and when he did move, it would have to be perfectly timed.

So he waited.

TWENTY-NINE

Roman, Lefty, and Donnie had to be careful not to run up on the back of Givens and the buckboard. On horseback, they were able to move a lot faster than the buckboard, so they had to stay back.

"We could go around them," Donnie said at one point, "and get there first."

"We could," Roman said, "but that ain't the plan, is it?"

"Besides," Lefty said, "we might get lost lookin' for them. We don't know if they're in a settlement, a house, or just camped someplace."

"Just be patient, Donnie," Roman said. "We'll find 'em soon enough."

"Oh hell," Lefty said.

"What?" Roman asked.

"Look."

Roman looked ahead of them and saw the buckboard listing to one side.

"Shit," he said.

* * *

"Shit!" Givens said as the buckboard leaned over.

Joe and Les dropped down from their seat and looked at the wheel.

Givens dismounted.

"What happened?" he asked, hoping the wheel itself hadn't broken. There was no way they'd be able to move on until they got another one from Gunnison.

"Dunno," Joe said. "We'll have to take a look."

"But the wheel itself is in one piece?"

"Looks like," Les said. "Come on, Joe. We should be able to fix this quick."

Givens watched as the two men slid beneath the wagon, and then he looked behind him. He couldn't see his three compadres, but he gave a helpless shrug anyway.

As he watched the two men work on the wagon, he knew it didn't matter how quickly they got it fixed. This would probably keep them from reaching their destination tonight.

He was going to have to camp on the trail with these two idiots.

Givens and the buckboard ended up stopping for the night well before Clint, Tesla, and Miranda had discovered their dead horse.

Roman, Donnie and Lefty were, therefore, forced to camp as well, keeping themselves well behind the buckboard so they wouldn't be detected.

By the time Clint and Miranda got back in the house after moving the horse, everyone on the trail had settled down . . .

Givens couldn't stand Joe and Les. They had more muscles than brains, and when they talked, the subject was always inane. He knew that he was often judged by his size, which worked to his advantage. Men usually didn't realize how intelligent he was.

But these two . . . they were as stupid as they appeared to be.

He sat off by himself to eat while the two of them chattered incessantly, food flying from their mouths. Givens was wondering about the merits of an idea. Maybe he should just kill these two and take the buckboard himself— except for the fact that they apparently knew where they were going.

He had tried a couple of times to find out their destination, but all they would offer was that they were following some directions they'd been given. So they didn't actually *know* where they were going, but they knew how to get there.

Givens ate and tried to block them out.

Roman poured himself some coffee and replaced the cast-iron pot on the fire.

"Givens must be going crazy," he said. "From what he said, those two ain't very smart."

"Usually men that big ain't," Donnie said.

"Except for Givens," Lefty said. "He seems pretty smart."

"Smart enough to kill anybody who disrespected him," Roman pointed out.

"Hey," Donnie said, "I give him all the respect he deserves. He may look dumb, but he ain't."

Roman put his coffee cup down and rubbed his shoulder.

"That arm hurtin'?" Donnie asked.

"Like a bitch," Roman said. "Reminds me why we're out here."

"I hope there's some profit in this," Lefty said. "I mean,

I know we're out here to get your revenge, but these fellas should have some money on them, or something on those buckboards."

"We'll take a look, once we've taken care of them," Roman said. "Hell, we walk away from this with both buckboards, we gotta be able to turn a profit."

Lefty and Donnie were happy that Roman was even thinking about making a profit. They were worried that his injury—and humiliation—might keep him from thinking about anything but revenge.

Clint left Miranda in the house with Tesla as he put the horses back in the makeshift stable.

"Don't worry, boys," he said, stroking both their necks, "we're not going to leave you out here alone."

He was taking first watch over them, even though the cat had the carcass of the dead horse to occupy it. Miranda was going to relieve him in four hours' time.

He built a fire in front of the lean-to, hoping that it at least would give the cat pause before it thought about approaching again.

It seemed like, with all the trouble they'd had with the three men at the settlement—whose number had somehow swelled to four—and the mountain lion, there hadn't been much indication that the original rumors about someone wanting to do harm to Tesla were accurate.

They had enough to deal with without that rumor turning out to be true.

The big cat moved closer to the horse's carcass. He could smell the scent of humans on the meat, but in the end his hunger got the best of him. He approached the dead horse and began to rip big chunks of meat from it, swallowing some of them whole in its haste to feed.

And all the while he was still aware that there were two more animals available to him.

The predator watched all the activity, and then when Clint settled down in front of the lean-to, he also settled back off his haunches, taking a seat. The fire was helpful. If he'd wanted to take the man with his rifle, he could have, but this man was not his prey. In daylight, when Tesla once again came out of the house, he'd be an easy target.

Beyond the house he could see movement as the big cat consumed the carcass they had dragged off. He felt a kinship with that cat.

They were both hunters.

They were both hungry.

THIRTY

Clint awoke as somebody approached him. He was sleeping in his bedroll on the floor, having given Miranda his room. She had offered him her bed when she relieved him, but he didn't want to feel her warmth on the sheets. He thought that—and her scent—might keep him from sleeping.

But it was Miranda who leaned over him and touched his shoulder.

"What—" he said, coming awake. "What's wrong?"

"Nothin'," she assured him. "Nikola was nice enough to come out and relieve me an hour early."

"Oh," he said, sitting up. "Why? Couldn't he sleep?"

"I didn't ask him for the reason," she said, taking his hands in hers. "I just figured we'd take advantage of the situation."

"Advantage?"

"Come on," she said. "My bed is much more comfortable than the floor."

She yanked him to his feet.

"Miranda—"

She pressed herself against him and kissed him. Her lush lips were hot and avid on his, her breasts pressed tightly to his chest.

"Come with me," she whispered, hooking her fingers into his belt.

He allowed her to tug him toward the bedroom, pausing only to grab his gun belt from a nearby chair.

"You really think you're gonna need that?" she asked.

"You never know," he said as she dragged him into the room and closed the door.

Tesla sat at the fire, looking at the sky as the sun came up. He had his rifle across his knees. It seemed to him he'd been holding the rifle in his hands since they left Denver, and yet it still felt foreign to him. He couldn't wait for the rest of his equipment to arrive so he could get started with his experiments.

He heard a sound off to the right and pointed his rifle that way. He held his breath, but nothing came out of the bushes.

Maybe it was just his nerves.

The predator saw Tesla sitting in front of the two remaining horses, knew that he was there to keep them safe from the prowling cat. But as the sun came up, the scientist was also making a perfect target of himself.

He decided to wait until the sun was high in the sky before taking his shot.

The cat circled around behind the man and sniffed the air. His muzzle was still red with the blood of the dead horse, and yet his hunger was unabated.

He didn't care if his prey was two legged, or four. He was ready to attack again, as the sun came up.

Inside the house, Clint undressed Sheriff Miranda Lawson, marveled at her body. Her breasts were large and firm, her waist small, her legs long and perfect. He turned her around and admired the firm ass and the deep dimples just above the cheeks.

He turned her back to face him, then took her into his arms and kissed her deeply, his hands roaming over her at the same time.

Impatiently, she yanked at his clothes, pulling them off him. They tumbled onto the bed naked, hot bodies pressed together, kissing feverishly. Neither of them realized how much they had wanted this from the moment they met.

Clint finally worked Miranda onto her back and began to explore her body with his hands and mouth . . .

The sun came up, and the predator stood, rifle in hand. He sighted down the barrel, and at that moment Tesla stood and stretched, presenting his chest as the perfect target.

As the predator moved his finger to the trigger, there was a sound behind him. Before he knew what was happening, the cat was on him, huge teeth sinking into the back of his neck. In moments the predator's neck snapped. His finger jerked on the trigger, and the rifle went off . . .

Clint had his face pressed between Miranda's thighs, lapping at the sweet juices that were flowing from her pussy, as the shot sounded. It was a single shot, loud and clear in the stillness of the morning.

"Wha—" Miranda said.

"A shot!" Clint said.

He leaped off the bed, grabbed his pants, shirt, and boots and yanked them on, then grabbed his gun and ran out the door.

Behind him Miranda did the same, just a bit more slowly.

Clint ran out the front door, knowing that a lot more could have happened during the time it took him to pull himself together. His shirt was open, his belt had been left behind. He paused, waiting for but hoping there would not be a second shot.

When it didn't come, he ran around the side of the house to the lean-to. At first he didn't see Tesla, but then spotted him. He was lying on the ground and not moving.

"Nikola!"

He ran toward the scientist, hoping that the younger man had not been killed while he was in bed with Miranda.

THIRTY-ONE

"Nikola!" Clint shouted, running to the fallen man.

As he reached him, the scientist moved, and stared up at Clint wide-eyed.

"What happened?"

"You tell me."

"I don't know," he said. "There was a shot . . ."

Miranda came running over with her pistol in her hand.

"What's going on?"

"I'm trying to find out," Clint said.

"Is he hit?" she asked, then looked at Tesla. "Are you hit?"

"I don't know—" He started to sit up, then stopped short. "Ow!"

"Let me see," Clint said. He pulled aside Tesla's jacket. "There's blood, but not much."

"We better get him inside," she said.

"You get him inside," Clint said. "I'm going to have a look around."

"Be careful."

"You, too."

As Miranda got Tesla up and helped him to the house, Clint looked around, trying to see where the shot might have come from. He decided a straight line was the best bet, and he started walking.

He smelled the blood before he reached it.

The body looked as if it had been torn apart. Blood saturated the ground, but the cat's prints were plain to see.

He found the rifle, a new Winchester with a handmade sight on it. A professional weapon. The dead man was either a soldier or a mercenary.

It looked like the rumor that somebody was going to try to kill Tesla was more than a rumor.

"What did you find?" Miranda asked as Clint entered the house. She was sitting in front of Tesla, who had his shirt off. He was very thin, with an almost concave chest.

"The shooter was torn apart by the cat. He had this." He showed her the rifle.

"How did he miss with that?"

"I'm thinking the cat hit him as he was pulling the trigger. How's Nikola?"

"Take a look."

Clint put the rifle down and approached them. Tesla had a scratch on his shoulder.

"The cat threw off his aim," Clint said, "You were lucky to get off with a scratch."

Miranda had finished cleaning the wound, and stuck a small bandage over it.

"Anybody ready for some breakfast?" he asked.

"Oddly, yes," Tesla said, shrugging into his shirt. "Coming close to death seems to have had that effect on me."

"It's called being happy to be alive," Clint said. "Bacon and flapjacks?"

"Sounds good to me," Miranda said. "Can I help?"

"You can keep an eye out the front window for a while," Clint said. "Just in case our friend had a friend."

"Okay," she said.

"Thank you for cleaning my wound," Tesla said.

"You're welcome," Miranda said, "but it was really just a scratch."

"It is my very first wound," he said. "Please don't take that away from me by calling it a scratch."

"Okay," she said. "I'll just say, 'You're welcome.'"

She walked to the window, picked up her rifle, and peered out.

When breakfast was ready, they gathered around the table.

"So the rumors were true," Tesla said. "The President was right to hire you to protect me."

"The President?" Miranda asked. "Of the United States?"

"He didn't really hire me," Clint said. "I sort of volunteered—and I didn't do a very good job this morning, did I?"

"I am still alive, aren't I?" Tesla asked.

"Yeah, thanks to that cat."

"Well, in that case, I hope you don't ever have to kill it."

"We'll have to wait and see on that."

"Any bacon left?" Tesla asked.

"I'll get it," Miranda said.

"Bring the coffee, too," Clint said.

She brought the pan with the bacon and the coffeepot back with her. Tesla ate the bacon that was left, and she poured coffee into everyone's cup.

"That buckboard should have arrived by now," Clint observed.

"Maybe they had trouble on the trail," Miranda said.

"Yeah," Clint said, "maybe human trouble."

"How will we know?" Tesla asked.

"Well," Clint said, "when you decide we've waited long enough, we'll have to go and look for them."

"What if there's somebody else out there with a rifle?" Miranda asked.

"Or that cat," Tesla said.

"I've been thinking about that cat."

"Thinkin' what?" Miranda asked.

"You hear those horses?"

"Yes," Tesla said, "I've noticed how restless they are. Is that because the cat is still out there?"

"Partially," Clint said.

"It's the blood," Miranda said.

Both men looked at her.

"The blood has soaked into the ground," she said. "The smell is makin' them nervous."

"That's right," Clint said.

"So what do we do?" Tesla asked. "How do we get rid of the blood?"

"We don't," Clint said. "Let's bring the horses around to the front of the house and tie them off. We can keep an eye on them that way. Also, they won't be able to smell the blood."

"They'll still smell that cat," Miranda said.

"Yes, they will," Clint said. "I might have to go out there and see if I can hunt it down."

"Alone?" Tesla asked.

"You'd be better off here with Miranda than out there with me," Clint said.

"What about the four men from town?" she asked. "You think they been hired to kill Nikola?"

"No," Clint said. "I think the one whose arm I broke is

out for revenge. The others are along for the ride to help him."

"Well," Tesla said, "when the rest of the supplies get here, we'll have two more men to help us."

"That's not what they hired on to do," Clint told him. "I doubt they'll want to be dealt a hand in this."

"So we will have to face them alone?" Tesla asked.

"Most likely."

"Can you handle them? The four of them?"

Clint finished chewing what was in his mouth, swallowed, and said, "I guess we'll find out."

THIRTY-TWO

"Stop!" Givens called.

The buckboard came to a stop and both men turned to look at him. Givens wasn't looking at them. He was looking up ahead.

"What is it?" Joe asked.

"Smoke, up ahead," Givens said.

They looked.

"Just a tendril," Les said.

"Probably coming from a pipe chimney," Givens said.

"That'd be our house," Joe said. "Should be right up ahead."

"Well," Givens said, "you boys better get going, then."

"Ain't you comin'?" Les asked.

"You said you was gonna help us unload," Joe reminded him.

"Well," Givens said, "I changed my mind. You just go ahead."

"Where are you goin'?" Les asked.

"You'll see me again," Givens said.

Joe and Les exchanged a glance, then shrugged. Joe snapped his reins and the team started up again.

Givens dismounted and sat.

Roman, Lefty, and Donnie came upon Givens a half an hour later.

"What happened?" Roman asked. "I thought you was goin' with them."

"I decided it might not be wise for me to go ridin' in there," Givens said.

"Why not?" Donnie asked.

"That lady sheriff," Givens said. "She mighta rode on ahead to warn them."

"You think they know we're comin'?" Lefty asked.

"Maybe."

"I wish I knew who that feller with the ax handle was," Lefty said.

"We shoulda drew down on him," Donnie said.

"He likely woulda killed you," Givens said.

"How do you know?" Donnie asked. "We don't know who he is."

"You three looked him in the eye and decided not to draw on him," Givens said. "He must be pretty damned good."

"Well," Roman said, "we're gonna find out how good."

"We'll wait here awhile," Givens said.

"Why?" Roman asked. "I can see that smoke up ahead."

"That buckboard will be just about there," Givens said. "Let's give them a chance to get involved in the unloadin', then we'll go in."

"Sounds good," Roman said. "Okay, dismount. We'll wait."

"Can we eat?" Donnie asked.

"Water and jerky," Roman said.

Lefty dismounted and said, "Looks like they might have some hot food up ahead, judging by that smoke. Bet it comes from an oven."

"After we take care of 'em," Roman said, "you can eat all the hot food you want."

Roman tied his horse and walked over to where Givens was sitting.

"You think I was afraid to draw on that man?" he asked.

"I don't know," Givens said. "I wasn't there."

"Well, I wasn't."

"Good," Givens said, looking up at him. "You'll get a chance to prove it."

THIRTY-THREE

They heard the buckboard before they saw it.

"What's that?" Tesla asked.

He was standing on the porch with Clint, watching the horses.

"Buckboard approaching," Clint said.

"It is about time," Tesla said, stepping down to the ground.

"Stop," Clint said. "Wait for them."

Tesla stepped back onto the porch.

Miranda came out.

"Buckboard," she said.

"We hear it," Clint said.

They waited. Eventually, the buckboard came into view as two men drove it into the clearing in front of the house.

"Mr. Tesla?" one of the men called.

"I am Tesla."

"We're from the Meridian Freight Company," the man said. "We have your supplies."

The two teamsters stepped down. They were large men

with muscular arms. One of them had a prodigious belly, which probably helped him with his heavy lifting.

"Would you like some coffee and something to eat?" Clint asked. "Before you begin to unload?"

They looked over at the first buckboard.

"Looks like a lot of work," one of them said. "Whataya say, Les? Breakfast first?"

The man with the big belly grinned and said, "Always."

"Come inside," Clint said.

He made them some bacon, coffee, and johnnycakes, because they were quick to make.

"Mighty fine meal," Les said.

"Agreed," Joe said, rubbing his belly.

"Why is the lady stayin' outside?" Les asked.

"The lady is the sheriff of Gunnison," Clint said. "She's looking after the horses, We lost one to a mountain lion."

"Maybe we can get some huntin' in, then," Joe said.

"After you unload my supplies," Tesla said. "I am eager to start with my work."

"Let's get started then," Joe said.

"Okay," Givens said. "Let's mount up."

The other three men rose and walked to their horses.

"How do you want to play this?" Givens asked as they started out.

"I want to kill them," Roman said, "both."

"But you want them to know it's you, right?"

"Right," Roman said. "I want to take that fella's ax handle and give him a taste of it himself."

"While we watch?" Donnie asked.

"While we keep our guns on him," Givens said.

"Suits me," Lefty said. "I ain't lookin' forward to facin' that feller with a gun."

"Why not?" Roman demanded.

"I dunno," Lefty said. "Just seems to me he'd be a hand with a gun."

"Because he can swing an ax handle?" Givens asked.

"He just makes me nervous, is all," Lefty said. "I'd just as soon get the drop on him."

"Let's ride, then," Givens said. "They should be in the middle of unloading."

THIRTY-FOUR

Clint helped the two men unload Tesla's heavy equipment. Tesla was too slight to be of any help, so he stayed inside and directed them where to put each piece.

Miranda stood watch over them with her rifle in her hands.

"What is this stuff?" Joe asked Clint as they walked from the house back to the buckboard.

"Just equipment," Clint said. "That's all I know."

"It's all metal," Les said. "Now we know why the damned buckboard was so heavy. We had to stop and repair a wheel twice."

"Axle problem?" Clint asked.

"No, radial."

"We fixed it," Les said.

As they were sliding another piece of equipment off the buckboard bed, Joe said, "Sure wish that other fella had stayed with us. We coulda used him."

Clint stopped. "Wait. What other fellow?"

"Huh?"

"What man are we talking about?" Clint asked, putting down his side of the equipment he was holding.

The two burly men put down their end of the equipment.

"Just a fella we met in Gunnison who was lookin' for a job," Les said.

"He was a big fella, so we figured he'd be a big help," Joe said.

"So what happened?"

"Couple of miles from here he quit," Joe said.

"Just like that?"

"Just like that," Les said. "He saw the smoke comin' from yer chimney."

"Miranda!" Clint yelled.

She came walking over.

"Tell her what the man looked like," Clint told the two teamsters.

They did.

"That's the man who came to see me, lookin' for you," she said. "That's why I came to warn you."

"Was he with any other men when you saw him?" Clint asked them.

"No," Joe said.

"And was anybody following you?"

"No," Les said, then, "nobody that we saw."

"Well, which is it?" Clint asked. "No, or not that you know."

They exchanged glances, and then Joe said, "Not that we know."

Clint looked at Miranda.

"They could have been followed," Clint said. "They just wanted these gents to lead them here."

"Is there gonna be trouble?" Joe asked. "We need our guns?"

"You might," Clint said, "but it would be better if we finished unloading and then you left. In fact, that might be what they're waiting for." He looked at Miranda. "We'll keep going, but keep a sharp eye out for anything."

"Gotcha."

"Gents," Clint said, "let's get moving."

Givens made them all dismount and move forward on foot. Before long they were able to see the house, the two buckboards, and the people.

"They're unloading, like you said," Roman commented.

"We take 'em now?" Donnie asked.

"No," Givens said.

"Why not?" Lefty asked.

Givens turned his head and looked at all three of them.

"They got two extra guns down there," he said. "That makes five. We go in now, we go in without our edge."

"He's right," Roman said. "We gotta wait until those two leave."

"You three go back to the horses," Givens said. "I'll keep watch and let you know when it's time to go."

"Suits me," Donnie said. "I'm hungry anyway."

"Jerky only," Givens said harshly. "No fire, no whiskey."

"Jesus—" Lefty said.

"Shut up," Roman said. "He's right. Now see if you can move without making noise."

The three of them drifted off, and Givens settled down to watch the activity in front of the house.

The big cat wasn't happy.

There were too many of the two-legged creatures around. He decided just to circle around and around, until some of them had gone away.

THIRTY-FIVE

The two teamsters had to stop and rest after unloading the first buckboard. Clint let them come inside, but suddenly the house was cramped while Tesla was assembling his equipment.

"Let's go back outside," Clint said.

They did, taking their coffee with them.

"So that fella we brought with us," Joe said. "He lookin' for you with bad intentions?"

"Real bad intentions."

"We're real sorry we brung him," Les said. "We didn't know—"

"I understand," Clint said. "Did he say anything to you on the way?"

"Nothin'," Joe said.

"He didn't talk at all," Les said.

"That didn't bother you?"

"Nope," Joe said. "We just wanted him for his size."

"Big?"

"Real big," Joe said.

"Bigger than us," Les said.

Clint looked at Miranda.

"Real big."

"Why don't you fellas go and check that other buckboard, see what we can take first?" Clint said.

"Sure."

As they moved away, Clint said to Miranda, "This big man, he's new. He wasn't with the other three when we tangled with them."

"So he must be pretty good if he's all the help they brought," she said.

"I guess so," Clint said.

Clint looked out into the trees.

"I ain't seen nothin' yet," she said.

"They're out there."

"How do you know?"

"Same way I know that cat is out there," Clint said. "I can feel them."

"Why don't we go out and get them?" Miranda asked. "We could go around back of the house and circle around."

"No," Clint said, "they're watching. If they don't see us, they'll know something is up."

"So what do we do?" she asked.

"Wait," Clint said, "we just wait."

They got the second buckboard unloaded without incident, but it was too late in the day for Joe and Les to leave, so they decided to spend the night.

"We can sleep in that lean-to in the back," Les said.

"You don't want to do that," Clint said. "A big cat killed one of our horses last night. The ground back there is saturated with blood, and that cat might come back."

"Thanks for the warnin'," Joe said. "We can sleep under the buckboards."

"Or in the beds, since they're empty," Clint said. "Might be better off doing that, with that cat still around. Tie your horses off next to ours right here in front of the house. With all of us bunched up here, it might discourage that lion from paying us a visit."

"What about the two-legged critters?" Miranda asked.

"We'll keep watch all night," Clint said. "I don't think they'll want to do anything in the dark. They'll still wait for Joe and Les to leave in the morning."

"Okay then," Joe said. "We'll get set up for the night."

"You're welcome to take supper with us inside," Clint said. He figured to cook the rest of the venison.

Givens realized the two teamsters were staying the night. He turned and walked back to where the other three were sitting.

"Get them saddles off," he said. "Them teamsters are staying' overnight."

"Why don't we take 'em in the dark?" Donnie asked.

"Yeah," Givens said, "why don't we break a leg tryin' to walk around this mountain in the dark? And why don't we run into the mountain lion whose tracks I saw on my way back here?"

"Lion?" Lefty asked.

"We're gonna have to build a fire," Givens said. "It'll keep the cat away, keep us warm."

"Can we cook?" Donnie asked.

"Yeah," Givens said after a moment. "Let's backtrack some. They're gonna be smellin' their own cookin' all night, but we'll put a little more distance between us."

"Plus we're downwind," Roman said.

"We'll set watches for the night," Givens said. "You three can take care of that since I watched the house all day."

The three men didn't argue. They all grabbed their horses' reins and followed Givens back along the trail a ways.

THIRTY-SIX

The two teamsters went to sleep right after their supper of venison stew and biscuits, and in moments they were snoring.

Clint stood out front with Miranda for a while.

"We still haven't had a chance to finish what we started," she said.

"I know," Clint said. "We might have to wait until we get someplace that has a hotel."

"I have a room back in Gunnison," she said. "You will have to go back that way to get off this mountain."

"Yes, I suppose I will."

The teamsters' snoring increased.

"I'm not gonna be able to sleep with all that racket," she said. "I'll take the first watch."

"Might not be as loud inside," he said, "but I won't argue."

She nodded and he went inside.

* * *

The house was now crowded with Tesla's equipment. Except for the kitchen and the table, there was not much room to move around—other than in the bedrooms.

"It looks . . . crowded," Clint said. He almost said "impressive," but he really didn't know whether to be impressed or not.

Tesla stepped back to view his work. His shirtsleeves were pushed up, revealing his stick-thin arms. He was breathing hard from exertion.

"Do you have everything where you want it?" Clint asked.

"Pretty much," Tesla said, "down here. But I must go up on the roof and connect these wires."

"To what?" Clint asked.

Tesla pointed and said, "The antennae must be erected up there. Remember you told me you would help?"

"I remember," Clint said. "We'll have to do that in the morning, when we have light."

Tesla looked unhappy, but said, "Very well."

"Tonight you should get some rest," Clint said.

"Yes," Tesla said, "yes, I am quite fatigued. What of our two new friends?"

"They're in the buckboard, snoring away," Clint said.

"And the lady sheriff?"

"On watch outside."

"For the cat?"

"For anything, and anyone."

Tesla approached Clint.

"Is there coffee on the stove?"

"Enough for a couple of cups."

"Good, then will you join me?"

"Sure."

Clint poured two cups and brought them to the table. The two men sat across from each other.

"So, Nikola, you have no idea who would have sent an assassin after you?"

"None."

"Edison?"

"I believe I told you the man is a scientist," Tesla said. "Scientists do not stoop to murder. I am afraid I would never believe that of him."

"Well, we can't be sure that whoever sent him sent only one," Clint said, "so we'll have to be on our guard."

"Seems we've been on our guard since we left Denver," Tesla said.

"Yes, well," Clint said, "sometimes that's the only way to stay alive."

"I would have to bow to your knowledge of these things," Tesla said. "Where will you be sleeping tonight?"

"I'll share the bedroom with Miranda," Clint said. "No point in leaving the bed empty."

"Good point." Tesla yawned, and Clint thought he heard the scientist's jaw crack. "I will turn in now with an eye toward rising early tomorrow. Hopefully, there will be some storms coming."

"Smells like it," Clint said, "but why do you want storms?"

"I need lightning for my experiments," Tesla explained, standing up and stretching. "I need to get those antennae up."

"Okay," Clint said, "first thing in the morning, then."

"After breakfast?" Tesla asked hopefully.

"Sure, after breakfast."

"Good night, then."

"Night."

Clint finished his coffee, then rinsed both cups out and stowed them away. He took a moment to study Tesla's equipment, some of the pieces as large as furniture. Other smaller pieces were joined together to form one large one. He finally admitted he didn't know what he was looking at, and went to bed.

THIRTY-SEVEN

Givens, Roman, Donnie, and Lefty sat around the fire. Donnie had been able to whip up a combination of beans and jerky, as well as a pot of coffee.

"I was just thinkin' about them smellin' our food," Lefty said.

"Hey, you wanted a hot meal," Donnie said.

"It don't matter," Givens said. "They know we're comin'."

"How do they know that?" Lefty asked.

"Those two teamsters surely told them about me," Givens said. "And that lady sheriff, she woulda recognized the description."

"So," Roman said, "they know you're comin'."

"They probably figure it's the four of us," Givens said.

"I ain't so sure," Roman said. "You're the only one anybody's seen."

"What're you getting' at?" Givens asked.

"I'm thinkin'," Roman said, "that you should ride in there alone tomorrow."

"And get my head shot off?"

"They ain't gonna shoot you right off," Roman said. "They're gonna wanna know what you want."

"And then what?"

"While you keep 'em busy, we work our way around behind 'em," Roman said. "Or better yet, we get 'em in a cross fire."

"And me, too," Givens reminded him.

"We won't start shootin' 'til you hit the ground," Roman said. "All you gotta do is keep them talkin', then hit the ground. It should all be over in no time."

"Says you," Givens said.

"You got a better idea?" Roman asked.

After a moment Givens said, "No."

"There ya go, then," Roman said.

"Maybe I'll come up with somethin' else by mornin'," Givens muttered.

"Well, you sleep on it while the rest of us keep watch," Roman said, "and if you come up with somethin' else, you can let us know."

Givens glowered at the three men, then rolled himself up in his blanket and went to sleep.

Clint woke up before Miranda could rouse him. He made a pot of coffee and carried two cups outside.

"Thought you might like one before you turned in," he told her.

"Thanks," she said. "I don't see nothin' out there, but it's like you said. I can feel somebody watching us."

"Could be them," Clint said, "could be that cat wondering why the horse smell and man smell are so close together."

"What about the female smell?"

"Maybe—if he's a male—he'll like that one most of all."

"Thanks a lot," Miranda said. She placed her left hand on his crotch. "Maybe he can smell that I'm in heat."

He slapped her hand away and said, "Stop that. What are our two friends going to think?"

"They're dead to the world," she said. It was true. Clint could hear the two of them snoring, competing to see who could be the loudest.

"We could sneak off to the bedroom," she said.

"That didn't work so well last time, Miranda."

She became serious and said, "I know. I'm sorry about that."

"Not your fault," he said. "Or it was both our faults. Pick one."

"Don't like either," she said. She tossed the remnants of her coffee out into the dirt. "Guess I'll go ahead and turn in."

"Good night," he said.

"Night."

She went back inside, leaving him alone with the teamsters snoring.

The cat circled wide enough so that he could see the four men sitting around a fire, and then the people at the house, bunched up together with the horses. There was no fire there to dissuade him, but one of the two-legged creatures was constantly moving around. The cat finally settled down, resting its muzzle on both front paws, and watched the house.

The cat also knew there was one more predator out in the trees, but seemed to instinctively know that the lone man was the most dangerous of all, and so decided to leave him alone.

The man with the rifle looked down at the house from his elevated vantage point. He had seen the result of the cat attacking his partner, had watched as Clint Adams found the body and took the rifle. Hopefully, Adams and Tesla would think there was only one assassin on the job.

The second predator had watched the buckboard drive in with the two teamsters, then became concerned when they spent the night. He didn't need to go against four guns in his quest to kill the scientist, Nikola Tesla.

He didn't know why he'd been hired to kill Tesla. In fact, he didn't even know who had hired him and his partner. All he knew was that he'd been paid half of the money up front, and had a job to do in order to get the second half of his payment.

He placed the stock of the rifle on the ground and leaned on the weapon. He knew the cat was around, but if it came near him, he was going to kill it. He believed the animal knew that, and would leave him alone. After all, predators recognized other predators, and knew to leave each other alone.

But even if he had to deal with the cat first, he'd never missed a target before, and he wasn't about to start now.

THIRTY-EIGHT

Givens awoke the next morning, told the other three to stay where they were. He rode back up to his earlier vantage point, walking the last hundred yards so his horse wouldn't alert anyone. He wanted to make sure the two teamsters were going to leave. They weren't gunmen, but anybody could fire a gun and get lucky. He didn't need two more guns going against them.

As he looked down, he didn't see anyone in front of the house. They must have all been inside the house, having breakfast. The horses had not yet been hitched to a buckboard.

As he watched, he saw the mountain lion come into view on the other side of the house. He was sand colored, one of the biggest cats Givens had ever seen. The cat stopped on the edge of the clearing, lifted his huge head, and sniffed the air. Givens watched with interest to see if the cat would move any closer.

The horses in front of the house shifted nervously as they smelled the nearness of the cat.

"What's that?" Tesla asked.

"The horses," Clint said. He ran to the door, grabbed his rifle, and stepped outside. He saw the cat, lifted his rifle, but he'd never seen anything that big move so fast, and it was gone.

Miranda came up behind him.

"What was it?"

"The cat," Clint said. "He's getting braver. He was coming closer until he saw me, then took off fast."

"What's he look like?" she asked.

"Big," Clint said, "real big. Biggest one I've ever seen—and fast."

"Then I'm not lookin' forward to going back to Gunnison alone when this is all over," she said.

If she was hoping he'd offer to go with her, he didn't bite. Instead, he said, "I don't blame you."

The two teamsters appeared behind Miranda.

"The cat?" Joe asked.

"I scared him away," Clint said, "but maybe not for long. You fellas better hook up your horses and get a move on."

"Don't gotta tell me twice," Les said. "I ain't lookin' forward to tanglin' with no cat."

They moved past Clint and Miranda and untied their horses.

Givens was surprised at how fast a cat that size could move. If he'd had nothing else to do, he would have liked to go and hunt that cat, test his abilities against the big animal. Maybe, after this was all over, he'd do just that.

The other predator watched the cat, wondering if he'd get close to the horses, or the house, but the Gunsmith appeared in the doorway with his rifle, and the cat recognized the danger and got out of there fast.

The predator was tempted to take a shot at Clint Adams right then and there, but decided not to alert the others. He knew that his first shot had to be at Tesla, just in case he got only one.

Clint stood guard with his rifle while Joe and Les hooked up their team.

"If you run into that fella who came up with you, and his friends, just keep going," Clint suggested. "I don't think they'll bother you."

"I hope not," Joe said.

"We got guns," Les said, "but we're not gunmen. We'll fight back, though, if it comes to that."

"If you hear shootin'," Joe said, "you'll know we didn't make it."

"Good luck," Clint said, "whatever you run into."

Joe snapped the reins at the team, and they moved off.

Tesla and Miranda came out behind Clint.

"We've only got one horse left for our buckboard," Tesla pointed out. "Will that get us back to Denver?"

"That depends," Clint said. "How are you supposed to get this equipment back to Denver?"

"I'm supposed to send a telegram to the company and let them know to come and pick it up."

"Were you planning on taking some back yourself?"

"Well . . . yes."

"Then I suppose we'll need to get another horse."

"You can get one in Gunnison," Miranda offered.

"Yeah, that's probably what we'll have to do," Clint said. "And I suppose we'll be loading some of it ourselves. We'll need some help."

"You can also get that from Gunnison," Miranda said. "Always a pair of strong shoulders for rent cheap."

"All right," Clint said. "Well, let's listen up and see if we hear any shots in the next hour. And keep your eyes open."

"Clint," Tesla said, "the roof."

"Oh, right," Clint said. "Miranda, Nikola and I have to put some stuff up on the roof. You keep an eye out."

"Okay," she said, "but don't fall off. With that big cat prowling around and all the guns, it'd be a shame for you to die that way."

"I'll be careful," Clint said.

THIRTY-NINE

There was no ladder anywhere. Clint used the buckboard to reach the roof and then haul himself up. Tesla handed up the antennae, then a hammer and nails. Tesla backed up so he could see the entire roof, then told Clint where he wanted each antenna.

In the distance dark clouds were gathering. The smell of rain was in the air.

"The timing was just right," Tesla said. "The storm clouds are coming in."

Clint straightened up and took a look.

"It'll be a while yet," he said. "I'll get the rest of these nailed down."

"Make sure they're firm," Tesla said. "We don't want any of them flying off when they get hit by lightning."

"Lightning?" Miranda asked.

"That's what Nikola Tesla is all about, Miranda," Clint said. "Lightning."

"Harnessing it," Tesla said. "Controlling it. Putting it to good use."

"You can control lightning?" she asked.

"I'm going to give it a good try," he said.

"There," Clint said. "That should hold them."

He climbed back down onto the buckboard, then stepped to the ground.

"No shots yet," he said to Miranda.

"I know," she said. "Maybe they got through."

"Maybe."

Givens heard the buckboard coming.

"Get out of sight," he told the others.

"Why don't we take 'em?" Donnie asked.

"What for?" Givens asked. "They don't have anythin' we want, and we want them out of the way. Get out of sight. We're gonna let 'em pass."

"Do what he says," Roman said.

They grabbed their horses and walked them into some trees, then waited. The sound of the buckboard came closer and closer, and then it passed. The two teamsters were holding their rifles and looking around, but they went right by.

After a few minutes Givens stepped out of hiding, followed by the others.

"Okay," he said, "they're gone."

"So now we go in?" Lefty asked.

"Not yet," Givens said, "but soon."

"Have you come up with another idea, Givens?" Roman asked.

"No," he said. "No, I've decided I like your original idea, Roman. I'll go in all alone. We'll just wait for the right time."

"When will that be?" Donnie asked.

"Don't worry," Givens said. "I'll know it."

* * *

The predator saw Clint walking around on the roof. If Adams had been his target instead of Tesla, he'd have been a sitting duck up there.

He sat back and watched as Clint erected some stuff on the roof. He didn't know what it was for, but there were some wires. Maybe they were putting up their own telegraph—except he hadn't seen any poles in the area. Well, he'd heard that Tesla was some kind of scientist. Maybe even a mad scientist.

Curious, he decided to keep watching. They may not have been on the roof, but they were all still sitting ducks. He could take them anytime he wanted to.

Anytime.

FORTY

The cat was territorial.

He'd made enough kills in the area to think that he owned it. He didn't like all the two-legged creatures that were wandering around. He'd had a taste of them and the horses, and he wanted more.

They were moving about now. If they would move away from the horses, he could dart in and grab another one for a quick meal.

He licked his muzzle and waited.

Clint went inside with Tesla, watched him fiddle with his equipment. There were knobs and dials, but at the moment they didn't seem to be attached to anything.

"They'll work once the antennae are hit by the lightning," Tesla said. "Then they're connected to these electrodes—"

"That's enough for me, Nikola," he said. "I think I'll wait for the real thing to happen, so I can see it for myself."

"That would be easier," Tesla agreed, "than trying to explain it to you."

"I'll just go back outside and stay out of your way," Clint said.

Tesla was already involved in his equipment before Clint even got out the door.

The predator sighted down the barrel of his rifle at the woman, then noticed the sunlight glinting off the badge on her chest. A woman sheriff? He wasn't aware that any law was going to be with Adams and Tesla at the house. In his head, his price just went up. If he had to kill a badge toter, that was going to cost somebody a *lot* more.

"Okay," Givens said, "I'll give you time to get around behind them, and then I'll ride in."

"What are you gonna do?" Donnie asked.

"Don't worry about it," Roman told him. "I'll tell you what to do."

The three men mounted up and rode out of camp. Givens took the time to stomp the fire to death, then mounted up and rode slowly toward the house.

As Clint stepped outside of the house, Miranda called, "Clint."

"Yeah?"

She jerked her chin and he looked in that direction.

"One rider," she said.

"I see him."

The man broke into the clearing and slowly approached the house. The other horses shifted uncomfortably. Clint doubted they were reacting to the rider. They had probably caught the scent of that cat.

As the man came closer, Clint asked Miranda, "Know him?"

"Yeah," she said, "he's the one who came to me lookin' for you in Gunnison."

"Looks like the one Joe and Les described, too," Clint said. "Okay, so something is finally going to happen."

"But what?" she asked. "Why's he just ridin' in alone?"

"I don't know," Clint said, "but I guess we're about to find out."

The predator with the rifle noticed the big man riding up to the house. He didn't know what the man had planned until he saw behind the house. From his vantage point he could see three other men moving in with guns in their hands. They were on foot, having left their horses behind.

Damn it, he thought, if one of them killed Tesla, he was going to lose his fee.

He sighted down the barrel, watched as the three men continued to move in closer.

"Hello there," Givens said, reining his horse in.

"Hello," Clint said.

"I remember you," Miranda said.

"Oh yeah," Givens said, "the lady sheriff. What are you doin' here?"

"I could ask you the same question."

"Me? Well, I tol' ya, I'm looking for a couple of men."

"And who might they be?" Clint asked.

"Well," Givens said, "if I ain't wrong, I'm thinkin' you're one of 'em. That means the other one must be inside."

"And you came here all alone?" Clint asked.

"Why not?" Givens asked. "It ain't like I'm lookin' for trouble."

"Well, I think you found some," Clint said. "Your three

friends must be coming up on the back of the house about now. The minute they make a move, you're a dead man."

"Now what kinda talk is that—"

"Mister," Miranda said, "seems to me you'd be better off finding out the name of the man your trackin' before you track 'im."

Givens frowned.

"What's that got to do with anythin'?" he asked.

"Allow me to introduce you," Miranda said. "This here fella is Clint Adams. That mean anythin' to you?"

Givens stared at Clint for a few moments, then shifted uncomfortably in his saddle.

"Clint Adams?" he said.

"That's right," Clint said.

"The, uh, Gunsmith?"

"That's right," Miranda said. "The Gunsmith."

Givens thought about Roman, Lefty, and Donnie coming up on the back of the house and said to himself, *Goddamn them!*

FORTY-ONE

The predator tightened his finger on the trigger, still sighting on the three men. One of them had his arm in a sling, so he decided to concentrate on the other two. He didn't know what their story was. Were they there for Tesla? Or the Gunsmith? Did they even know who they were sneaking up on?

And was the big man out front with them? Or were they simply taking advantage of the distraction?

He picked his target, and aimed at him.

"I'm assuming you're here to distract us while the others work their way from behind," Clint said. "I've got to tell you, you won't live to see if this plan works."

Givens wet his lips.

"N-Now wait a minute, Adams," he said. "Nobody tol' me you was here."

"That's not an excuse for trying to kill me," Clint said.

"No, no," Givens said, "I didn't come here to kill you."

"Then why are you here?"

"Roman," Givens said, "you broke his arm with an ax handle. H-He just wants to get back at you."

"So he's creeping up behind us with his two friends?" Miranda asked.

"That's right," Givens said, "Lefty and Donnie."

"And you're just here to help them," Clint said. "Maybe hold me down while they do some damage with an ax handle."

"No, no, no," Givens said quickly, "I was just comin' to make sure everythin' was, ya know, fair."

"And you're in favor of things being fair, right?" Clint asked.

"Sure," Givens said, "sure I am."

He wished he had the nerve to draw on the Gunsmith, but he didn't. Jesus, what if he killed him? What a reputation he'd have. Maybe if Roman and those other two idiots would show up . . .

"I know you're waiting for your three friends to show up," Clint said, "but I've got to tell you, you're going to catch my first bullet."

"Now, wait a minute—"

"I think I hear 'em comin' now," Miranda said.

"You take that side," Clint said to Miranda, "and I'll take this."

"Right."

Givens sat his horse, still trying to work up the nerve to go for his gun. If he was on his feet, if he and Adams were facing each other with no guns, it would be different. There wasn't a man alive who could stand up to him in a fight.

He waited for his chance.

The predator switched his target.

The big man on the horse was probably the most dangerous of the four. That was probably why he went riding straight to the front of the house. He saw Clint Adams and the lady sheriff split the sides of the house. They knew about the others, and were ready.

He moved the barrel of his rifle and sighted on the broad back of the man on the horse, and waited for the action to commence.

FORTY-TWO

Clint waited for the men to come into view before he removed his gun from his holster.

Miranda held on to her rifle. Not being as adept as the Gunsmith was, she needed to be ready.

Roman wondered for a moment why he didn't hear any voices. Givens was supposed to keep them talking. Just for a moment he thought he should wait, but then he drew his gun.

"Go ahead," he told Donnie.

As Lefty came around the other side of the house, he saw Givens still sitting his horse. The odd thing was, Givens never went for his gun. Lefty took a few more steps, and found himself looking down the barrel of Miranda Lawson's Remington.

"Shit!" he said.

Miranda saw the man appear with a gun in his hand and didn't hesitate. If he was just some innocent man wandering around the mountain, too bad.

She shot him.

Clint saw the man with the gun come running around the house and recognized him as one of the three.

Donnie saw Clint, recognized him as the man with the ax handle.

The man's gun was still in his holster. Donnie grinned and raised his gun.

"No ax handle now," he said.

"Don't need one," Clint said.

He drew and fired.

Roman heard the shot and saw Donnie step back, and then fall onto his back.

"Donnie?"

Two more steps and he'd see what was going on in front of the house.

But he stopped.

Tesla heard the shots and came to the door.

"What is happening?" he asked.

Clint turned and shouted, "Nikola, get back inside!"

Then he heard the sound. A bullet striking flesh. The sound of the shot came later.

The big man on the horse swayed, frowned, and fell from his saddle. He was bleeding from a huge hole in his chest.

Tesla looked down at the body.

"What—"

"Inside!" Clint said. He rushed forward and pushed Tesla inside and closed the door.

A bullet struck the door and punched right through it.

The predator fired, struck the big man dead center in the back. He knew his bullet would punch right through. He ejected the spent shell, inserted a fresh one, then saw Tesla in the doorway. He fired a split second too late. Adams had shoved Tesla inside and the bullet had struck the door.

"Damn!" he swore.

"What's going on?" Miranda asked.

She looked down at the fallen man, and at the size of the hole in him.

"What did that?" she asked.

"Sharps," Clint said, "Big Fifty."

FORTY-THREE

"Inside!" Clint yelled again, this time to Miranda. "Before he reloads."

She ran to the door. He pushed her in, ran in behind her, and slammed the door.

"What is happening?" Tesla asked.

"There's another assassin," Clint said.

"But the shots . . ."

"We took care of the others," Clint said. "Actually, with the help of the assassin. He shot the big one."

"We're missin' one," Miranda said.

"Right," Clint said. "The one with the broken arm."

Suddenly, it became dark out.

"The storm clouds are coming in," Tesla said.

"Where is the assassin?' Miranda said. "You said he's firing a buffalo gun?"

"Yup," Clint said. "Could be from three or four hundred yards away."

"Well, our guns are no good at that distance."

"Let me see your Remington," Clint said.

She handed it to him.

"Yeah," he said, "I could get him with this, but I'd have to know where he is."

"How you gonna make a shot with that?" she asked.

"I know of a man who made a shot with a Remington at four hundred yards."

"What if he's farther away than that?"

"Then I'll have to get closer," Clint said.

"What do we do?" Tesla asked.

"You stay inside," Clint said. "Miranda, I need him to take one shot so I can locate him."

"So you want me to be the target?"

"I don't *want* you to be."

"I can do it," Tesla said.

"No," Clint said.

"Yes," Tesla said. "Why would he shoot at her? He doesn't want her. He wants me."

Clint looked at him. He was right. If Miranda stepped out, the shooter would ignore her. Clint wasn't sure why he'd shot the big man. Maybe he was afraid he'd lose his prey—Tesla. So it was only Tesla who could draw him out and get him to take another shot.

"All right," Clint said.

"You can't let him do that," Miranda said.

"You'll have to help me spot him, Miranda," Clint said. "You stand at one window, me at the other. When you see the muzzle flash, call out. I'll get him."

"What if you miss?"

"I won't."

The shooter kept his rifle trained on the door. The storm was coming in behind him. He had to make the shot now. He'd waited too long, and now was in danger of losing his prey. If only his partner hadn't gotten careless, they'd have worked this together.

He was going to take one last shot from here, and then move in closer.

Tesla walked to the door.

"Ready?" he asked.

"I'm ready," Miranda said at one window.

"Wait," Clint said, standing at the other window. He broke out the glass with the rifle stock. "Okay, ready."

Tesla opened the door.

Behind the house, Roman wasn't sure what to do. Running was an option, but he was still mad. Even if the others were dead, he had a chance for his revenge.

There was no back door, but there were back windows. If he could get in that way, he could take them from behind.

He approached the back of the house, then heard the growling noise.

He turned quickly and saw the cat.

FORTY-FOUR

Clint had an idea of where the shots might have come from. If he'd been the one with a Sharps, he knew where he'd position himself.

Tesla had his hand on the door, so Clint put his finger on the trigger.

Tesla held his breath and opened the door. His instructions were to stand still, count to three, and then drop down, but he found himself curiously staring out into the distance, wondering where the shot was going to come from.

Clint had explained that with the weapon they were dealing with, the bullet would reach them before the sound of the shot.

"Nikola, down!" Clint shouted.

Tesla dropped just as a bullet punched through the door.

"I saw it—" Miranda shouted, but Clint ignored her. He saw it, too.

He sighted down the barrel of the Remington. The cloud cover didn't help. There was no sun to reflect off any metal. By the same token, there was no sun in Clint's eyes.

He saw him. The man had stood to make the shot, and that was his undoing.

Clint fired.

The predator heard the shot, even saw the muzzle flash, but was convinced he was out of range. He was about to shoulder his Sharps for another shot when something punched him in the chest. Curious, he looked down and saw the blood.

How? he wondered.

His last thought was, *Damn, that was a good shot!*

"Did you get him?" Miranda shouted.

"I got him," Clint said. "Nikola, you okay?"

"I am fine," Tesla said, "I think."

At that moment they heard the commotion from behind the house.

"Back window!" Clint shouted.

When Roman saw the cat, he froze.

The animal was huge, and Roman knew it could be on him in seconds with its long strides. His only hope was that the animal would decide he wasn't really that good a meal for him.

With his right arm in a sling, there was no way he'd be able to pull his gun in time left-handed.

He stared at the cat, hoping the animal would see something in his eyes that would change its mind.

Apparently it did see something in his eyes.

Fear.

The cat moved.

Roman screamed.

*   *   *

When Clint got to the back window, he saw the cat tearing into a man. He could see the sling around the man's neck, so he knew who it was.

Miranda joined him and said, "Oh, God."

Tesla stood behind them, looked between them, and said nothing.

Clint backed up, broke the window, and stuck the muzzle of the rifle out.

The cat reacted to the sound of breaking glass, turned, and ran off before Clint could get off a shot.

Clint turned and ran for the door.

"Where are you going?" Miranda shouted.

He stopped at the door and turned.

"I've got to track that cat," he said. "He's grown too accustomed to the taste of human flesh. We won't have a moment's peace unless I get him. Also, I've got to check on the shooter, make sure I got him, see if there's any sign of still another assassin."

"Let me come—" Miranda started, but he cut her off.

"You've got to stay here and watch over Nikola," Clint said. "I'll be back as soon as I can."

As Clint went out the door, Tesla called out, "But what if you don't come back?"

"Don't worry," Miranda said, "he will."

FORTY-FIVE

Clint found the tracks of the cat very easily and began to follow them.

He knew he was taking a big chance leaving Tesla with Miranda. There was still a small chance that she wasn't what she said she was, and might have been a third assassin. But he was a pretty good judge of character, and he didn't feel that was the case.

He was sure he had hit the assassin with his shot, but had no way of knowing whether or not it was a killing shot. He was going to have to find the body to be sure he was dead.

As luck would have it, the cat was leading him in that direction.

Miranda and Tesla got together and moved the bodies away from the house—first the three in the front, and then what was left of the one in the back—just in case the cat decided to come back for an easy meal.

After that, Miranda insisted they go back inside to wait. She made a pot of coffee, then stood at a window holding the cup in her hand, the rifle leaning against the wall within easy reach.

Tesla wanted to work on his equipment, but was still too keyed up by the day's events.

"It is going to rain for sure," he said, joining her at the window.

"Yup."

In the distance they could hear the rolling thunder, and see the flashing lightning.

"Will he be able to track the animal in a storm?" Tesla asked.

"I don't know," she admitted. "I don't know how good a tracker he is."

"Well, I hope he can do it soon," Tesla said. "I will not be able to concentrate while he is out there."

"I know how you feel, Nikola," she said. "Believe me, I know how you feel."

Clint knew the storm was rolling in. The cat, also knowing a storm was coming, was probably going to ground. Clint had to get to that cat before the lightning and thunder started and the animal found shelter.

Eventually, Clint came to the shooter. The Sharps was lying on the ground, loaded for another shot. The man was lying on his back. Clint's bullet had hit him dead center in the chest. He had died quickly, hadn't bled much. The cat had not gotten to him. Clint turned the man's face to him. He had never seen him before. He went through his pockets, but there was nothing there to identify him. The man was too professional to carry identification.

He finished examining the body, picked up the Sharps.

Then, just like that, the hunter became the hunted. He knew the cat was out there, watching him.

He put down the Sharps Big Fifty, picked up Miranda's Remington. Slowly, he stood up. The rain started to fall. In moments, it was going to be dark—very dark.

He thought he could smell the cat's wet fur.

Then he heard it. A low growl. He squinted, held the rifle ready. Would it come for him? Did it want to end it now, just like he did? He was convinced that these animals had intelligence—high intelligence. But did they *think*?

"Come on, come on . . ." he muttered.

The cat came, just as there was a clap of thunder and a flash of lightning.

It came from behind.

Miranda jumped at the first thunderclap.

Then the lightning came.

"Excellent!" Tesla yelled.

She turned from the window.

"Did it work?"

"It will," Tesla said. "As soon as the lightning hits one of the antennae."

"Then what will happen?"

"These tubes will light up," Tesla said. "The electricity from the lightning will be in here"—he pointed to his equipment—"and I will have control of it."

"You'll control the electricity?"

"Yes."

"And then what will you do with it?"

He spread his hands and said, "Anything I want."

Clint turned in time to see it coming, but not in time to get off a shot. It seemed to be flying through the air as the lightning flashed again. He tried to bring the rifle around, but the cat hit him. He went sprawling one way and the rifle flew another.

The cat landed, then turned and looked at Clint over its shoulder.

Clint reached for his pistol, but as he did, his hand brushed the Sharps, lying on the ground. With his handgun, he'd have to hit the cat a couple of times, or more. But with the Sharps, one .50-caliber shot would do it.

The animal turned and glared at him.

His hand closed over the Sharps.

The cat tensed, preparing to jump again.

Clint picked up the Sharps, brought it around as the cat pounced.

He pulled the trigger.

FORTY-SIX

The rain was coming down in sheets.

The lightning kept coming, but for some reason had not struck any of Tesla's antennae yet.

Miranda had stopped waiting for that to happen. She was standing at the window, waiting for Clint.

It had been two hours since he'd started out after the cat.

"I don't understand," Tesla said, walking around the room. "We should have had a strike by now."

He stood in the center of the room with his hands on his hips.

"Wait!" Miranda said.

"What is it?"

"There he is! It's Clint."

She ran to the door and opened it. Clint came running in, carrying two rifles. He was dripping wet. She slammed the door behind him.

"Are you all right?" she asked.

"Yes, yes," he said. "I'm fine. Just wet."

"Did you get . . . it?" Tesla asked. "The mountain lion?"

"Yes," Clint said, sitting at the table, "I got it."

"And the other man?" she asked.

"He's dead."

"So it's all over?" Tesla asked.

"For now," Clint said, "unless someone else is sent to kill you."

"Two men and a mountain lion," Tesla said. "I think that is quite enough."

He turned and walked back to his equipment.

"What's going on?" Clint asked Miranda.

"The lightning hasn't hit his . . . things."

"Oh."

"You should get those wet clothes off," she said. "Why don't you go into the bedroom?"

"Yeah," he said. "I'll need a towel and then I'll change."

"Good," she said with a smile. "We were waitin' for you to come back and make supper."

A week later they all went back to Gunnison for supplies. They hitched Miranda's horse to the buckboard along with the remaining team horse. When they arrived, the first thing Clint did was buy a second horse. They left the team and the buckboard at the livery, which was housed in a large tent.

They decided to spend one night and then head back the next day.

Miranda found Tesla a place to stay. They were in the saloon, at the bar, each holding a beer.

"You can have a tent," she said to the scientist, "with or without a girl."

"Girl?"

"A prostitute," she said. "Do you want one or not?"

"Not tonight, I think," he said. "I need to think, to figure out what went wrong."

"Okay," she said. "I'll get you a tent . . . alone." She looked at Clint. "I already have a place for you to stay. Wait here for me."

"Okay."

"See you in the morning," Tesla said, and followed Miranda out.

In Miranda's tent they rolled a blanket out on the floor and rolled around naked on it. Clint reveled in Miranda's full, round breasts, sucked avidly at the large nipples, licked the wide aureoles. It had been a while since they'd been interrupted, and both were tired of waiting.

Clint had nothing against whores, as long as he wasn't paying them. Miranda was no longer a working girl, but the skills she had honed while plying her former trade had not eroded. She slid down his body, using her mouth and tongue to trace a trail, and when she arrived at his crotch, his penis was hard and raging. She took it in one hand and let her mouth swoop down and take it in. She sucked him wetly, taking him all the way in, then letting him slide free. She licked the bulging head of his cock, licked the shaft, then took it back into her hot mouth. Meanwhile, one hand circled the base of his cock while the other hand fondled his balls, and probed even lower.

Before long he was arching his back, lifting his hips off the blanket, and exploding into her eager mouth . . .

"Wow," he said as they lay side by side on the blanket, "you must have been good at your former job."

"I was a very good whore," she said.

"Why'd you quit?"

"I got tired of it," she said. "I decided I'd only lie with a man when I wanted to—like with you."

"And the sheriff's job?"

"That was a whim," she said. "I was crossing the street, saw the badge, picked it up."

"And when did someone come to town to talk to you about killing Nikola?"

She turned her head and looked at him.

"You know about that?"

"I suspected," he said, "but you confirmed it just now. I just couldn't see why else you'd come all the way out there."

"You're a sneaky man," she said. "Yes, a man carrying a Sharps came to town and talked to me about it. He offered me a lot of money to help him."

"Pay you in advance?"

"Nope," she said. "He was supposed to pay me after."

"Why didn't you kill him when you had the chance?" he asked. "When I went after the cat?"

"I like him," she said. "And I like you. I guess you can say the two of you kinda talked me out of it."

"I had a feeling about you," he said. "That's why I left you alone with Nikola."

"You took a chance that you were reading me right."

"I don't see you as a lawman or a killer, Miranda."

"Then what, should I go back to being a whore?"

"I think you should move on and do whatever you want to do."

"I can't," she said.

"Why not?"

"You killed the man who was supposed to pay me."

"Did he say who was paying him?"

"No," she said.

"Well, that part wasn't his job. That was what Jim West

was working on. Did he say anything about anyone else?"

"He had a partner, but you killed him first," she said. "As far as I know, it was just them two."

Clint reached over, put his hand on her flat belly.

"You're a beautiful woman, Miranda. San Francisco loves women like you."

"Like I said," she told him, "no money."

"I'll stake you, and I have some friends there who own hotels and would be glad to put you up . . . for a while."

"And what will they expect in return?"

"That'll be up to you and them," he said, "but I'll present you as a friend of mine."

"You would do that for me?"

"Yes. But I want you to go right away," he said. "Next time Nikola and I come here for supplies, you better be gone."

"Oh, I will!" she said eagerly. "And will you come to San Francisco and see me?"

"You bet I will," he said, sliding his hand lower. She had a wild tangle of pubic hair, and he wrapped his fingers in it.

She rolled to face him and said, "Well, let me give you something else to make sure you remember me . . ."

The next morning Clint hitched the new horse up to the buckboard, next to the old one.

"I always wonder how they get along when they are hitched together so closely," Tesla said, entering the livery.

"They know their jobs," Clint said. "You ready to go?"

"I think so."

They walked the buckboard outside.

"Did you manage to figure out your problem?" Clint asked.

"Not really," Tesla said as they climbed onto the seat together, "but there's another storm coming soon. I should have it figured out by then."

"Well," Clint said, "I'm fairly certain nobody else is going to try to kill you, so you should be able to concentrate with no interruptions."

"Are you sure?"

"Pretty sure," Clint said. "Maybe the problem was with me. Maybe I put those antennae on the roof wrong." Clint felt he needed to give the young man a way out.

"Hmm, that could be," Tesla said. "Perhaps they need to be slanted in a certain direction . . ."

"Yep," Clint said, snapping the reins, "perhaps they do."

Watch for

THE LETTER OF THE LAW

361st novel in the exciting GUNSMITH series
from Jove

Coming in January!

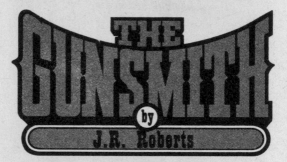